D0338565

The LAST MAN at the INN

The LAST MAN at the INN

R. WILLIAM BENNETT

ENSIGN
PEAK

Library of Congress Cataloging-in-Publication Data
Names: Bennett, R. William, author.
Title: Last man at the inn : one man's quest to believe / R. William Bennett.
Description: Salt Lake City, Utah : Ensign Peak, [2019]
Identifiers: LCCN 2019020001 | ISBN 9781629726038 (hardbound : alk. paper)
Subjects: LCSH: Jesus Christ—Fiction. | Bible. New Testament—History of Biblical
    events—Fiction. | Jews—Fiction. | Christians—Fiction. | LCGFT: Bible fiction.
Classification: LCC PS3602.E66449 L378 2019 | DDC 813/.6—dc23
LC record available at https://lccn.loc.gov/2019020001

Printed in the United States of America
Lake Book Manufacturing, Inc., Melrose Park, IL

10   9   8   7   6   5   4   3   2   1

To all those who seek:
Press on.
I can assure you that you will find
and it will be opened unto you.
He promised.

Author's Note

This is the story of one man's spiritual journey, a journey that millions of others have taken. The setting makes the tale thought-provoking and engaging, but the real story is about this man's change of heart.

Profound and serious research—both ancient and recent—has refined our understanding of the birth and life of the Savior. The census that brought Joseph and Mary to Bethlehem is questioned by credible historians as perhaps being a simple way to explain some other convention of Herod. It is speculated, with some reasonable evidence, that Joseph and Mary resided for some time in Bethlehem before Jesus was born and that the star may not have been evident until months or even a few years after his birth. These and many other discoveries continue to shed new light on the details of this most sacred event.

However, because the intent of this book is not to teach history, science, or politics but to explore a change of heart, I have decided to use traditionally accepted elements of the Savior's birth as the backdrop for this story to appeal to your familiarity and make the most important discovery for the reader not historical facts but spiritual truths.

I pray it will touch your heart, strengthen your faith, and bring you closer to our Savior.

PART 1

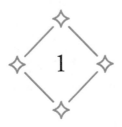

1

The traveler hunched over his lamb stew. For a moment, the noise, the heat, and the others at the table all disappeared from his consciousness as he took his first bites of the warm broth. Having a room for the night was an unexpected pleasure; but a hot meal prepared by someone else was a complete luxury. Not three hours before, he had been on a futile search for lodging in Jerusalem. Now, here he was in Bethlehem in what was likely the last accommodation in the area.

Normally he would have embraced sleeping under the stars on the outskirts of whatever town he found himself in; but the crowds here brought with them many who would try to rob a man in the night. Having a room at an inn would allow him to sleep without worry.

A merchant for thirteen years—if he counted the ten spent traveling with his father—the man regularly followed a half dozen trade routes in this part of the Empire. He knew that at certain times of the year, Passover especially, one did not try to stay in Jerusalem. And now there was also the census! Everyone traveling everywhere to get to their place of birth. There was not a single room left in Jerusalem. He had tried all his regular places, attempting to leverage relationships he and his father had built over the years, but nothing was available. Some of his old friends told him they felt terrible, as if they should have known he was coming. Of course, this was not possible. The life he lived revolved around unpredictable timing: when goods became available for a merchant to purchase, how well the travel went, how long his supplies lasted, and more. As he searched, many householders—their spare rooms crowded with travelers—laughed at him. He began to feel naive for thinking he could come during the middle of the census and just secure a space. "Foolish!" one man shouted at him before briskly shutting the door in his face. After that, he too kept repeating the word, over and over, castigating himself for his ignorance. *Foolish, indeed!*

After giving up in Jerusalem, the traveler decided to push himself to walk another two hours to Bethlehem on the slim chance that something would be left there.

The walk was hard; and the road was packed with hurried crowds making their way to Jerusalem. At first, as he led his train of donkeys through the oncoming hordes, he tried to tell the people he passed that they would not find anything ahead of them. A few said they would be with family, but most just ignored him. *People can be so stubborn,* he thought to himself. He listened as the animals around him brayed in protest, perhaps sharing with each other grievances similar to his own. But he pressed on, the search for a room now becoming more a matter of not letting the situation beat him than assuring a safer resting spot.

As he approached Bethlehem, he noticed clusters of sheep scattered across the hillsides as far as he could see. Some shepherds listlessly moved their flocks; others just sat in the late-afternoon sun, watching the travelers on the road. Their lives were not affected by this Roman census. Most had been born in Bethlehem and had never left, so they had nowhere to travel to; but even if they had, they could not leave their flocks. Any calls to be counted would be ignored. Should the census takers want to count the sheepherders' numbers, they could come find them.

The man also noticed a number of exposed caves along the ridges of the hills. Most appeared to shelter not the usual animals but families. This was not a good sign. It doubtless meant that, here too, any available rooms were long gone.

The traveler entered the town and soon began inquiring about a space, receiving the same scornful replies he had in Jerusalem. A small village, in fact no more than a rise on a hillside, Bethlehem was not popular. Under most conditions, there would have been plenty of availability for those who thought they could save a few shekels by staying here rather than in the Holy City. Of course, the man knew this was more ignorance on their part, as the savings were hardly worth the long and difficult walk to Jerusalem. However, Bethlehem was the city of David, and when the census began, the small village seemed to attract anyone who felt it could enhance their standing to claim it as their place of birth. Therefore, the streets were teeming with people and animals.

He had almost decided to go into the fields to see if he could find a corner of a cave to sleep in, when he heard yelling nearby. Just to his left was a doorway. Someone came staggering out, yelling incoherently. A large man followed him, shouting back.

"Get out!" the big man yelled. "You know the rules! You are in my home! With my family, no less! You want to be drunk? Go out with the goats!"

The man who had been tossed out stumbled and fell toward the traveler, who caught him. The man smelled strongly of wine and pushed back to start wobbling down the street. The traveler quickly realized his good fortune and stepped through the door at once.

"I see you may now have a single opening," he said.

The large man, who was clearly the master of the house, looked perturbed. But then he smiled. "Your timing seems providential. There is a place, just one. You will share the room with others, but it's a space, and you may join my family for a meal in a few minutes. Have you an animal?"

"I do. Three donkeys."

"There is a pen around back. Put them up and then come in for some stew. Your name?"

"Simon."

Simon walked his pack animals through the narrow side alley to the pen, already home to three or four other animals. He led his donkeys in, added some hay to the bin, and took the bags filled with spices off each animal one by one. When he carried the bags into the inn, the large man looked up and, without a word, nodded his head toward where Simon would sleep. Simon dropped the bags in the small alcove that would be his home for the night. A low table had been set, and a family with two children sat on the floor at one end. Next to them were two young boys, perhaps twins, that must have been the sons of the householder. Simon paused for a second, the pang of missing his wife surging through him. He had not been married long, and they were slowly adapting to these long absences. It was the merchant way of life, just as it had been with his father, and one had to accept the challenges that came with it. Simon sat on the floor at his place, putting as much space as possible between himself and the others.

The patriarch of the little family at the other end of the table acknowledged him with a silent nod and continued talking to his wife and children in hushed tones.

As with most inns, this was primarily the home of the man who had granted him the space. The main floor was normally constructed to be just a stable, covered by the rest of the house. However, many had converted the keeping area for animals into a large open room where they could let out space to travelers. On the next floor up would be family living quarters for the owner.

Soon the innkeeper's wife came to his side and ladled some stew in the empty bowl before him.

"It is good to have so much need for rooms, but sometimes . . ." Her voice trailed off as she shrugged her shoulders and shook her head.

Simon thanked her and contemplated his stew for a moment. He savored the steaming bowl by holding his face over it, letting the moist heat waft up his cheeks.

After his first bites, his annoyance at the whole situation returned. *This census*, he thought. It created such a turmoil, and he did not understand why everyone should travel all these different places to be counted. If they were simply counted where they were, the number would be the same. But, like most Jews, he had resigned himself to the idea that living under Roman rule had many inconveniences—some severe, others not so much. To be fair, there were advantages too. The Roman road system and sea traffic had entirely changed travel. Rome had established a consistent monetary standard that allowed all her subjects in all her provinces and kingdoms to trade easily. But all this notwithstanding, when someone wanted something they could not have or was asked to do something they didn't want to do, it was always easiest to blame the Romans.

Simon was born a long distance from Bethlehem and had decided that wherever he was when the census takers confronted him would become his birthplace. More than likely he would be on the road, and they wouldn't bother him. One fewer person and three fewer donkeys in the count would not matter to anyone.

Simon was a Jew, but he kept his religion in a manner driven by convenience. He was a decent and honest man. He worked hard. He'd married and had a young wife. They had a baby on the way. However, he saw no need for the traditions and trappings of his Judaism unless they helped him. Or his wife insisted he keep them. When traveling, he kept the sabbath if he was tired and ignored it if he needed to work. He observed the kashrut diet if those foods were available but ate what he wished if they were not or—when not at home—they did not seem appealing. He prayed if he had needs, asking for help. He did not bother God when he had control of his situation and needed no divine intervention. He felt he did the truly important things right and did not let the rest bother him.

He took another bite of his stew, the warm meat comforting him. He had been eating quietly for a short time when he noticed the owner of the home walk to the door and speak softly to a young man about his age, possibly younger. Simon leaned back to peer through the open door. The young man had a donkey, upon which sat a very pregnant woman. Simon watched as the older man kept shaking his head, politely at first but then more insistently when the younger man raised his voice slightly, pleading. Simon looked around the small room. The family he was sharing it with were oblivious to the discussion at the door. The quarters were tight, and there really was not room for an additional person, let alone two. He shifted his glance back to the open door. The householder, who clearly wanted to help the young man, turned and locked eyes with Simon for the briefest moment. He knew what was silently being asked of him. And he answered back just as silently by returning his gaze to his meal. The young man continued to plead as the master of the house sadly and softly closed the door, blocking the young couple from view. Once more, he looked at Simon, and Simon thought he saw a fleeting moment of judgment, but then the man shook his head and returned to serving their guests.

Ignorance, Simon thought to himself. *To think they could get space; in fact, space for two! What did they think coming at this late hour? Foolish.*

Then something came to his mind. He thought of his upbringing, of his mother teaching him how to be a good person. He thought of how generous his father had always been when they traveled together and came across someone in need of food or drink.

He shook his head, trying to rid it of the thought. But it was like a bothersome fly, and it would not go. *Perhaps,* he thought,

I should give up my space. The woman was pregnant. It would be the thing my mother would have expected me to do, the thing my father would have done. Thoughts of Mara, his wife, and the baby she was carrying entered his mind. He had a brief pang of guilt. But then he found his defense: "I am exhausted, and I deserve a decent place to sleep." Apparently he had said it out loud, as the family looked up to see if he was addressing them.

This self-affirmation enabled him to sit still, to lay claim to what was his; but not, as he had hoped, to find peace from the nagging impressions.

2

Simon finished his meal and went to his mat to lie down. It was too early in the evening to retire to bed, and he knew he should not do it, but he could not keep his eyes open. When he awoke, he could tell it had been dark for hours. He heard hushed whispers coming from the father and mother just feet from him. Their talk was of nothing too personal: how long they would be in Bethlehem, thoughts about their children. Though their conversation did not seem private, he did not want to appear to be listening. He also knew he would not fall back to sleep unless he went out for a walk.

He quietly slipped out of the house. The streets were peaceful, the only sounds that of animals in nearby pens and stables. The sky was clear, the air cool. He loved this time of night, though he was rarely able to enjoy it. After a long day of walking or negotiating with the market vendors over his goods, he usually went to bed at dusk and was almost always tired enough to sleep through the night without waking.

As he walked, he passed many who, not as lucky as he, slept on the street, leaning against the walls. A few startled as he passed and looked his way, perhaps frightened that he was out to rob them. He did not like disturbing people, so he turned down a road toward the open fields.

Out here it was even more peaceful. In the moonlight, he could see the herds of sheep were now clustered in larger groupings along the rolling hills. The shepherds brought them together at night to make them easier to guard. He found a path that led by one of the many ridges with exposed limestone caves. In each one, he could see by the light of the dimming fires inside that they were filled with people. Most were lying on beds of hay, sleeping, but a few were up, stoking their fires and perhaps keeping watch over their families.

Then it hit him.

Looking back toward the flocks, he noticed there were no shepherds. *Where were they?* For a shepherd to leave his flock untended was the ultimate act of irresponsibility. A shepherd who was an owner would never leave them, and a hireling only if he did not fear the punishment that would come for having done so. Shepherds were entrusted with the care of their defenseless animals, and offering that protection was their only reason for being. But as Simon continued walking, he saw the same thing again and again.

He was not as much troubled as he was curious about what had drawn them away. Seeing nothing that answered his question, however, and feeling that he could now sleep again, Simon decided to follow the path back to his lodgings. Then, just as he was about to do so, something caught his eye. He looked back, scanning the view in the moonlight. There in the distance was another cave; but unlike the others, this one had several people congregated around its entrance. He walked closer to get a better look. Sitting, standing, and kneeling were shepherds—at least a dozen of them, old and young. They were quietly staring into the cave. He didn't want to approach the crowd. If there was any attention directed toward him, he might be drawn into whatever was going on and lose his chance of getting enough rest for his journey tomorrow.

Just the same, he was curious. Walking in a wide swath and keeping his distance from the cave, he crept through the rocky field until he could see inside. What he saw caused him to freeze in his tracks.

Carefully, he took a few steps forward, squinting to confirm what he thought he'd just seen. Two steps more. Another.

He paused and caught his breath.

There in the cave was the couple he had seen pleading for a room at the inn just hours before. Simon felt a growing discomfort. He moved closer yet again, in tiny steps, one arm back, as though he could pull himself away should he get too close. There was the young woman, resting on some hay that had been propped up just so to make a spot for her. Simon moved carefully from side to side until he saw what he was searching for.

There! In her arms—a child! A new child, born this very evening. He was mesmerized by the scene. Certainly he had seen many children before, including those as young as this. Birth was awe-inspiring. But why the fascination of the shepherds, who had uncharacteristically left their flocks? As he pondered this, he had an experience unlike any before it. It was a thought—no, not a thought. It was something more—an affirmation, perhaps? Suddenly he knew something he had not known just seconds earlier. He did not know how he knew it, but he knew he knew it: this was different. There was a peace here that was more than quietude, more than respect, though both were palpable. This was something else. This was *holy*.

Though he was not a religious man, he recoiled from the thought. It felt . . . sacrilegious. Things holy were somewhat foreign to him; but, still, he was loath to call something holy that was not. Holy things were in the synagogues, in the scrolls, and with the priests burning incense in the temple. This was just a cave, a mere peasant woman and man, and a baby just like millions before him.

Yet, there! It came again.

And with it came comfort, a reassuring feeling that it was acceptable for him to think this way. He felt unsure, confused, and captivated all at once.

He stood for a while, lost in his thoughts, until one of the shepherds turned and saw him. With a kind look, the man beckoned him to come forward. Simon waved his hand back and forth almost imperceptibly. He was not sure why. He was . . . what? Uncomfortable somehow? It felt inappropriate for him to go nearer. It was not the newness of the birth, in which a mother should be given privacy. It was . . . well, he was not sure what it was.

Suddenly, shame swept over him. He realized that this woman had given birth in a cave, on a bed of hay, surrounded by animals. He remembered the thought he had had earlier that he should give up his space for them—the thought he had worked so hard to force from his mind at the time. Certainly a mat on the floor of the householder's home would not have been much more comfortable than this, but at least it would have been more private; and the mother staying there with her family would have been able to assist with the birth.

That was it! He felt guilty . . . but also unworthy somehow of moving any closer. Then another thought hit him: *Go forward. Just for a moment. Speak to the man and his wife and apologize for not taking the opportunity to make them more comfortable.* But he did not move. He looked at the ground, shame bubbling up within him. No, this was his place, out here. He did not deserve to get any closer.

Still, the thought persisted—*Go to the man, ask if there is anything you can do for him and his wife.* Perhaps the master of the house had some stew left; he could run and get it for them! Perhaps they could use a shawl, as the night would likely get cooler; he could spare one of his extra robes! His spices! One could be used to mix with oil to anoint the child.

But he did as he had done before; he forced himself to start back. *I am so tired,* he repeated to himself, *and I need to be on the road in the morning. I need my rest. They have had a baby and seem comfortable enough. If they need anything, I am sure they will ask one of these shepherds.*

He took several steps and then paused to gaze back over his shoulder for one last look. He could no longer see inside the cave, but the fire illuminated some of the shepherds' faces in its entrance. On the far right of the growing congregation was a young boy not more than twelve. Tears rolled down the boy's face, glistening in the firelight.

Again, he felt the urge to approach the cave. And again he

denied himself. He spoke out loud to provide extra will: "I need to go back into town."

He walked quickly toward the lodgings, as though he could outpace his discomfort. He *had* felt something. It appeared all the shepherds had as well. But what had they seen that he had not? What was so powerful that they had left their responsibilities behind? Was he more disciplined because he had made himself return? Or was he more shallow because he had not been enveloped by what seemed to have a hold on them? He felt a strange sense of loss.

It was far from the first time he had encountered this kind of dissonance. Most often, the feeling came when he passed a beggar. The man or woman would plead for money. Simon nearly always had money, but it troubled him to give it away, and he rarely would. Furthermore, he doubted his coins would make a difference. And even if they could, there were still so many beggars on the street. If he helped one, shouldn't he help them all? When would it end? And didn't they bear responsibility for being in that state? Wasn't their condition a result of their own lack of industry? Wouldn't it be better for them to work themselves out of poverty than for him to assist them in staying in it? In time he developed a strategy when encountering beggars on the streets. He would set his sights straight ahead, eyes in front of him. If a vagabond called out to him, he would pretend not to hear. It felt a little uncomfortable, but he didn't know what else to do. In fact, this habit had become his resolution for all things he did not understand: he ignored them. Ignoring such things, he believed, would free him from vexing issues—his existence would remain unclouded by troubles.

So, with practiced skill, he pushed the troubling thoughts from his mind on this unusual evening, and when he reached the house, he went quickly to his bedroll.

But sleep did not come.

3

The next morning Simon walked out to feed his animals and prepare them for the day's long journey back through Jerusalem and on to Jericho. But when he looked out at the street, he was surprised to see crowds pulsing in every direction.

He rarely sold his wares in Bethlehem, where the villagers were less wealthy than those two hours up the road in Jerusalem or a day ahead in Jericho. To meet the needs in Bethlehem required him to lower his prices. But with the morning's overflow from the Holy City, there appeared to be many who would make time spent here more lucrative than usual.

Simon retrieved one of his saddlebags, slung it over his shoulder, and walked to the square, which was teeming with merchants and townsfolk. He quickly found a man selling spices and approached him. The man's bins were nearly empty, and the marketplace was crowded. These were perfect conditions! The man would see Simon's leather bag and know exactly why he was there.

This was where Simon was wrong. The merchant, who was hurriedly speaking with several other men, turned, gave Simon a quick glance, and then returned to the anxious conversation.

Simon was surprised. "You!" he said firmly, trying to get the man's attention. "I have spices to sell. You appear to be nearly out. Would you like to buy more?" The man looked at his bins with surprise, then up at Simon somewhat apologetically.

"Of course. Sorry. Just a moment." And one more time he turned to his group of friends.

Simon was shocked. In just the few minutes he'd been there, he had watched several people walk up to the table expectantly, observe the smatterings of spices left in the bottoms of the baskets, and then quickly move on to find another seller. He too moved on.

As he walked through the marketplace, searching for another spice seller, he noticed that many of the other merchants also seemed to be lost in hushed conversations with each other while barely registering their customers' presence. In a crowd like this, good sellers should be calling out their offerings and watching prospective buyers like hawks. The best merchants would be aware of twenty people at once, noticing even the most imperceptible turns of the head or split-second lingering looks, and then calling the person out, drawing them to their table. Today, however, everyone was preoccupied.

Just when his thoughts were about to give way to verbal exasperation, Simon heard, "Sir, you need spices? I have a good assortment."

Simon looked to see who had spoken and saw what must be the one man who had managed to stay focused. He walked to the table, and the man looked pleased, fanning his hands over his baskets.

"I don't need to buy spices, but I have them to sell. Do you need to replenish?"

The man was momentarily disappointed, but then he looked in his baskets and shrugged his shoulders. "If you have anise, and perhaps cinnamon. Nothing else, and not too much."

Simon took the bag off his shoulder and reached in, finding the right pouches. He and the merchant engaged in the typical haggling to agree on a price. Simon usually enjoyed this, for he was good at it, but today it gave him greater pleasure because it was the first thing so far that seemed to work as it was meant to.

Simon tucked his earnings into his pouch and, as he did so, said, "May I ask you something?"

"I need nothing else," the merchant came back quickly. "And please stand aside. I cannot see through you."

"Of course," Simon said, then walked around the table. The merchant gave him a confused look but turned to a new customer who had just come forward. Simon waited patiently, and after the person left, he asked, "Your fellow merchants. They all seem engaged in some deep conversations. They are missing buyers . . ."

"To my advantage," the man said, never taking his eyes off the passersby.

"What is it they are all talking about?"

The merchant paused and glanced at Simon, looking at him as if he had just asked where Bethlehem was. He turned back to the crowds but spoke to him.

"You must not be listening. It's all foolishness, but people love a foolish tale. Look how it turns them from what they should be doing."

Simon tried to encourage him. "I know. I've seen it often. What is it this time?"

The merchant shook his head with a look that resembled something between pity and disdain. "They talk of the prophecy from the scriptures. They all think the baby was born here last night."

Simon waited in silence for more information.

Again, the merchant glanced at Simon, but this time he lingered longer, looking at him from top to bottom. "You look like a Jew. Are you not a Jew?"

"I am a Jew," he answered simply.

"Not a good one, then," the merchant said as he smiled and turned back out to watch the crowd. "Sir!" he called out. "Are you in need of spices? I have fresh spices!"

The skilled merchant was successful, and again, Simon waited while the transaction was completed.

"I may need some more of your spices after all. Your presence seems to be good for business. Stay here with me longer," the merchant said. Then, without missing a beat, he continued as though it was part of the same thought: "A good Jew would know the scriptures, even a little."

Mockingly, he continued. "Let me think. What prophecy was that, the one about the baby being born who would save the Jews? Hmmm, I know I've heard about that somewhere . . ."

Simon knew the prophecy. And it wasn't that he didn't want it to be true, but things were what they were, he often said. Rather than wait on a distant hope of being delivered from the Romans, he had long ago learned how to live under Roman authority, going along with the rules rather than chafing against them. He was not sure he believed in the prophecy.

"This baby they talk of—they think *this* baby is the prophesied King?" Simon chuckled. "And born in Bethlehem?!"

The merchant looked at him angrily, surprising Simon. "Yes, Bethlehem. The city of David, or didn't you know that, either?" he said derisively.

"I am sorry," said Simon. He had forgotten that part. "I meant no offense. It was just surprising to me for a moment. Of course, this *is* the city of David. Still . . . a king . . . ?" He trailed off.

The merchant transacted another sale, then turned to him. "Quickly, is there more cinnamon?"

Simon retrieved another pouch, saying simply, "I should charge you more, but it will be the same."

The merchant quipped back, "You should charge me less, but it will be the same."

The merchant jostled the basket of freshly added cinnamon, dusting the air with its scent to entice passersby.

"As for me, I believe the prophecies. But, this . . . this is not the fulfillment. These people, they are so tired of the"—he lowered his voice—"the Romans. Anything that happens, they say, 'This is a sign,' as though talking about it will bring it sooner."

Simon cocked his head. "You don't believe in signs, then?"

"No, I believe. But the King would at least be born in the nicest house in town, not in a cave."

Simon froze. He replied cautiously, trying to sound nonchalant. "In the caves? The caves east of town?"

The merchant stopped and eyed him suspiciously. "There are caves every direction from town. It was indeed in the caves east of town. You must have seen this birth, then?"

Simon shrugged. "I live far from here. I don't know the area, but I saw caves to east when I arrived, so that is what I was asking." That was not a lie, so he was able to say it easily. He added another truth, one that was, in its incompleteness, designed to deceive: "I did not see any birth."

The merchant lingered in his stare, then looked back to his business. "Yes, in those caves. Supposedly many shepherds left their flocks. The people are saying this was a sign." He laughed. "It's a sign, all right. A sign that those shepherds are irresponsible. And here is my prophecy . . ." In a serious tone, he leaned forward and said, "I foresee they will lose their sheep." He chuckled at his own wit.

Suddenly his demeanor changed. "Sir, you have been entertaining, and I appreciate the spices, but I am weary of this. I cannot think of two things at once. I need to tend to my table."

Simon thanked him and said goodbye. He began to search for others who might be interested in his herbs and spices, but as he wandered the market, he did not put much effort into finding any buyers. Instead, he drifted close to some of the other conversations, trying to listen in. But when the whisperers noticed him, they would cease talking and stare until Simon moved on. He understood now why everyone was conversing in hushed tones. Everyone, including Simon, knew that when there was unrest in the communities, Herod would send out spies and guards to listen and learn. These spies, nearly everyone believed, reported back to Herod, who took swift action against anyone who seemed the least bit out of line. Herod maintained peace at any cost.

4

By evening time, Simon had decided he would leave the next day for Jericho. He had been tempted to stay in Bethlehem and take advantage of the crowds, but he knew he would still sell all he had in the long run, so there would be no loss in leaving.

At dinner, after making small talk with the other guests, the owner of the inn walked over to Simon and sat across from him on the floor. "You have seemed deep in thought. I have more stew to offer you, but I thought I would wait until you asked me. You haven't, so I thought I would check before I give the rest to my sons."

Simon looked up from his bowl. "Yes, thank you. I'll be on my way tomorrow, and the extra would be appreciated."

The man stood and retrieved a ladle, dipped it in the pot, and carried it without a drip to the table, where he poured it into Simon's bowl. He sat again.

"I don't mean to bother you, but you seem troubled. Would you like to share what concerns you?"

Simon did not move, nor did the man. Finally, Simon looked up. "Yes, I've been trying to remember something and I am a bit embarrassed to ask you for help. I'm afraid it will say more about me than I care to share."

"We are all on a journey," said the man. "Where I am and where you are does not matter, only that I may help you in the direction you wish to travel. What is it?"

This was unusual, to find someone so helpful. Simon looked at him, felt his humility, and decided to trust him.

"Well," Simon began, "I am a Jew."

The man laughed out loud. "Really? And here in Bethlehem? How strange!"

Simon smiled. "Yes, but I am not done. I am a Jew, but I don't keep our ways too diligently. I have been sitting here trying to remember the words in our scripture that refer to the prophecies of a king being born in the city of David who would come to save us. Try as I might, I cannot recall them."

He looked up sheepishly.

The man pursed his lips and nodded slightly. "You have been listening to the talk, then?"

"I did hear it. Yes. But that only got me thinking about it. I thought it would be good to recall exactly what has been taught." He paused, then quickly added, "It's not that I think this baby is the King."

The man cocked his head, "And why not?"

Simon was surprised. "I am sorry, I'm not trying to challenge whatever you feel."

"Oh," he replied quickly. "You didn't bother me. My question is sincere. I am just curious why you are so sure this child is not the King."

Simon thought about his answer. "I don't know for certain. It's just that . . . a cave . . . Bethlehem—not that there's anything wrong with your city . . ."

The man smiled. "Stop worrying so much. I am an Idumean. And . . ." The man looked over his shoulder at the other family, lowered his voice slightly, and with noticeable sarcasm, said, "According to these sons of Jacob, I am not a *real* Jew. If I was taken aback by insult, I would spend my life going backward." He laughed at his own joke, then became pensive again. "So, I ask you again, why are you so sure? Is that so much more fantastic than, say, the parting of the Red Sea? How about manna? Jericho? All these things are quite fantastic, are they not? The birth of a baby seems trivial compared to these miracles, and a baby must be born somewhere. Why not here?"

The man smiled, lifting his eyebrows and waiting for an answer he knew would not come. He laughed, then leaned forward, folding his large arms in front of Simon.

"A child is born unto us, a son is given unto us; and the government is upon his shoulder and his name shall be called Wonderful Counselor, Mighty God, Everlasting Father, Prince of Peace. That the government may be increased, and of peace there be no end, upon the throne of David, and upon his kingdom, to establish it, and to uphold it through justice and through righteousness from henceforth even forever." He then slapped Simon's forearm warmly. "That was our prophet Isaiah speaking, my friend."

And without another word, he went back to his business.

5

Simon rested better that night. In fact, he rested better than he had in a long time. He was quite perplexed about the talk surrounding these last two days. But, somehow, when he slumbered, he fell into a state of peace he had not known for ages. Was it the stew? The cool evening air? Perhaps it was thinking about Isaiah's prophecies. Whatever it was, he was grateful. He felt refreshed and renewed.

He stepped out of the home quietly and was surprised to see the householder.

"Did I wake you?" Simon asked.

"No, no. You didn't," the man replied. "I just wanted to speak with you before you leave. Would you allow me to speak boldly?"

"I am not sure you know any other way," Simon said wryly.

The man laughed. "See, we are friends already." He then became more serious and looked Simon in the eye. "I feel I need to tell you—I know you are searching for something. I believe it is not a coincidence that you were here in our village at this time. I believe you were led here, to this village, and to my home, for a reason. My friend, seek out that reason. It is important. I feel it."

Simon was annoyed. Whatever was going on his heart, which

even he did not seem to understand, was his business. He walked deliberately past the man and said, "Thanks again. It was pleasant staying in your home," not giving time for response.

"Shalom," he heard him say. He turned to reply, but the door was closed, the householder having disappeared behind it.

Soon, Simon had loaded his things and was walking north, out of Bethlehem.

6

Simon's work required that he make his way from a port city to inland markets and back again, sometimes walking more than twenty miles in a day. As he traveled, he never failed to appreciate the good Roman roads and sea traffic. The Romans had crisscrossed the Empire, building well-paved highways that made travel quick and painless. And in each port city, Roman ships came and went multiple times a day, carrying everything from everywhere to everywhere. A traveler need wait only a few hours, and he would have an opportunity to pay passage to any place accessible by what the Romans called Our Sea.

As common conventions had evolved, the whole system worked even better. When he left his home, Simon would pay a camel owner to carry his packs of spices and herbs down to the shore, a journey of ten miles. He would find a ship going the direction he wished to travel and make arrangements. When he landed at his desired city, he would disembark, purchase donkeys or camels, and begin his journey selling. When he was done, he would reverse the process: meet incoming merchants like himself, sell them his animals and sometimes even his empty bags, and then board a ship for home. When he arrived back home, he would make the half-day walk up the into the hills to return to his family.

This day, he was on that last step. As he approached his village, he was met at the outskirts of town by little children, always excited to see newcomers. Upon recognizing him, they ran to him. A few were nephews and nieces who jumped up to hug him; others were simply their friends who thought the leap and hug looked fun and joined in.

"Aaron!" he said as he swung his nephew from side to side. He put him down and got on one knee. "Would you do your uncle a favor?"

"Yes!" the young boy squealed, feeling quite important.

"Run ahead and find Mara and tell her I am back. It will be more exciting if she knows I have arrived and comes out to greet me."

He started walking again, this time more slowly to give Aaron time to find Mara. By the time he passed through the village gates and came to the first street, Mara was walking up to him, arms outstretched. She wrapped her arms around his neck, kissing his cheek. They stood there, and then he leaned back, surveying her. He was shocked at her protruding belly. He knew it would happen, but he still stared in amazement. She smiled as she held her hand beneath her stomach.

"I'm glad I'm not later!" he said. "Will we have time to get back to the house?"

She laughed. "You man," she said derisively but jokingly. "Yes, we will. We have at least a week. I was so hoping you would make it back in time to be with me."

They locked arms and walked back to their home.

It was a humble place. In fact, it was just a room in a building that housed several other one-room abodes. It had been partitioned with a small table to one side, a place for their bed at the other, and—always a little disconcerting to him—a small, carefully kept shelf, almost shrine-like, on which Mara kept their Sabbath candlesticks.

Mara was devout. He'd known that when they married. They never discussed it, though. As it seemed with most couples, one person was more devout than the other. It's just that she was more devout than most and he less so. When he wasn't traveling, they observed the Sabbath together and ate according to the commandments, but only because she ensured they did. He loved his wife—dearly—and all this was worth it to please her.

Another feature of their home was a small stairway inside that led to their roof. On warm evenings, it provided a cooler place to sleep. He and Mara enjoyed sitting there after sunset, looking at the sky and talking. Tonight, they did just that and were fortunate they had the space to themselves.

They had eaten earlier, and she had caught him up on the unimportant but interesting events that had transpired in their village in the three months he'd been gone. He shared a few stories of his own travels. They then talked of names for their baby.

Then, after a comfortable period of silence, he said, "Something interesting happened when I was in Bethlehem that I want to tell you about."

She turned toward him with great effort. "Bethlehem? You never go there. What took you to Bethlehem?"

He shook his head. "The census. Apparently, nobody lives in the town of their birth. The entire population seemed to be going somewhere else all at the same time. There was no room for me in Jerusalem, so I moved on to Bethlehem and, even there, got one of the last places to sleep." He paused and got more serious. "There was a child born while I was there."

She laughed. "It is good to know that life goes on in Bethlehem. I believe there were children born in many places that night."

"Yes, I suppose so. But this one was . . ."

She waited. "Yes?" she prompted him.

He searched for the words. "This one . . . was typical but seemed to attract such attention. It was a young couple, younger than us, who must have been having their first child. They were travelers to Bethlehem, I suppose for the census. They tried to stay in the pace where I was, but I had gotten the last space . . ."

She stopped him. "You saw them?"

"Yes, of course. That's how I know they tried."

"You saw she was pregnant?"

He stopped. He was so intent on getting to the core of the story he did not realize he had just incriminated himself. He knew what was coming next.

She waited before she spoke. "You know what I am going to ask you."

"I do. I still feel guilty. I cannot believe with you pregnant I was not more unselfish. Another night under the stars would not have hurt me. It still bothers me."

She said nothing else but patted his hand lovingly and looked back at the sky as he continued.

"Anyway, they eventually found a cave. There are dozens of them there, and it seemed each one had travelers in it. I know this because that night I went out for a walk, and I passed their cave and saw them."

"How could you be sure it was them?"

"That's what I want to tell you. Normally I would not have been able to tell from a distance, and honestly, would not have cared. But I happened upon this cave, and out in front were at least a dozen shepherds, just quietly staring into the opening."

She sat up, swung her feet to the ground, and turned toward him. "Go ahead."

There was something she seemed to be listening for.

"Well, they were just looking. There were animals about too. I suppose this cave served as a pen for a local man. There was a cow, the donkey they had ridden, and some sheep."

"I don't need to know about the animals!" she said.

"It's part of the story. They—the animals, the shepherds—were all quiet. They were just looking in. I didn't want to get close, so I stood at a distance and walked until I could see in. There was this couple, and the woman had obviously just given birth, and she was holding the baby."

Mara still watched him intently.

"I am not sure why it was so unusual. The quiet, I suppose. The shepherds not with their flocks in the middle of the night— that was strange. But more than all that, it was just . . . peaceful somehow. It was like they, and for a minute me as well, were removed from the rest of the world. It was almost like I was in a synagogue."

The two of them sat there quietly for a moment. When he said no more, she said, "I think there is more?"

He had no idea how she did his. When he was with her, his thoughts seemed to be written on his face.

"Yes, the next day I was in the marketplace selling my spices, and everyone seemed preoccupied talking about this birth. I hesitate to even repeat what they said—it seems almost inappropriate. But they kept saying it was the fulfillment of prophecy."

"It is," she replied simply.

"You know this?" he asked. Then he felt foolish again. Of course she knew it; she listened to the scribes.

Either his wife did not want to embarrass him or she was lost in thought. She stared but seemed to be seeing nothing. Suddenly but softly she just started speaking: "'A child is born unto us . . .'"

She turned to look at him, eyes moist. "That's the one," she said quietly.

He sat back and stared at the wall around the edge of the roof. He was filled with feelings of inadequacy. Inadequate that he did not know this prophecy well. Inadequate because he could not quote more than a few verses of scripture. Inadequate that this remarkable woman had married him, clearly a sacrifice for her.

She seemed to read his thoughts. He felt her hands on his cheeks, gently turning his head toward her. "I love you," she said, "and I love that you love me. I feel blessed every day."

They sat quietly for a while, arms entwined and hands clasped, just pondering. Their heads were only an inch from each other, but he supposed their thoughts were miles and miles apart: his focused on his shortcomings, hers, perhaps, in Bethlehem.

7

Seven days after Simon's arrival home, early in the morning, Mara asked him to run and find the midwife. When he returned just minutes later, he heard his wife trying unsuccessfully to stifle her groans of pain. The midwife, an older woman with whom no woman or man would argue, opened the door to their home, entered, and pushed him back out in one fell swoop. There was no explanation needed. He was a man, and his place was outside.

He sat on the ground, leaning against the wall. He could hear most of what was going on inside and became disturbed when he heard the midwife's voice grow suddenly anxious. She ordered the young girl that had come with her to get something. The girl came rushing out and ran a few doors up the street to her home, went in, and came out no more than a minute later, running back toward him.

He stood to block her way. "What is it?" he demanded. But the old woman had trained the girl well. She said nothing, just dodged him and ran into the home with whatever it was she carried.

"What is it?" he yelled into the house.

The midwife yelled back. "Quiet! Leave us alone."

He again sat on the street, knees up, as he leaned against the house. Suddenly he had a thought. He clasped his hands and rested his arms upon his knees. He put his head down for privacy. He spoke softly.

"Dear, God," he uttered, speaking waveringly, "I am not a good man, and I do not know you. But my wife, you know her well, and I am asking you if you would help her. Whatever is wrong, would you . . ." He paused about to use a word he rarely used. "Would you . . . *bless* . . . her? Bless her, please. She is a good woman, a better woman than I am a man. I know you are all-powerful and can do anything. Would you please protect her and our baby?"

He had not realized he was crying, but as he raised his head, he felt tears run down his cheeks.

A moment later, he heard the midwife begin speaking in soothing tones. "That's it, that's it, that's it. Perfect, Mara!" He heard Mara offer a short scream of effort, and, then, there it was. A baby began to cry.

He did not hear Mara, but he listened intently to the midwife. Her voice was calm, if not happy. And then he heard Mara laugh and cry at the same time.

He stood and started to push open the door.

"Not yet!" the midwife managed to yell in between her soothing expressions of affirmation to Mara. He took his hand off the door but kept his ear close to hear.

Several minutes later, the midwife opened the door. "I did it." And without looking at him, she started up the street, women running to her to hear the news.

He heard his wife call to him. He stepped in and walked carefully to their bed. She was weary, her hair sweat-stained and her eyes tired but glistening. She saw him looking at her and motioned with her head to look down. Against her chest, a perfect baby was held tight.

She looked up. All she said was, "A son."

He was in awe. He reached out to stroke the little head but stopped short and looked inquisitively at Mara.

She laughed. "Of course you can. He is your son. You won't hurt him."

He touched him. His skin was so soft that somehow the word *soft* seemed insufficient. His features were perfect, and he could see that his little nose turned up just like Mara's. He kept staring, looking for words that would not come, words he did not even seem to know.

This morning there had been one person he loved beyond words. And now, where there had been one, there were two.

Suddenly he saw the image of the cave and the child the shepherds had gathered to see. He contrasted the two experiences—that night and this morning. They were different, but they were connected too.

There had never been anything more perfect to him.

8

Eight days later, in the temple, the rite of circumcision was performed, and their son was given a name: Alexander.

It was an unusual name for a Jewish son, though not unheard of. And despite what others thought, Simon and Mara both loved the name. Simon stayed with Mara and Alexander for as long as he could, but after a month, they could not afford for him to be without work. They needed the money, and so Simon reluctantly left again, with a promise to Mara that he would make the trip as short as possible.

Perhaps it was the birth of his own son that made him pay such close attention, but it seemed everywhere he went on his travels, he heard talk of only one subject—the child born in Bethlehem. He listened attentively but never revealed that he had been there at the time; and he certainly did not divulge the guilt he carried. As he thought of Mara's situation at Alexander's birth—comfortable in her own home, the midwife just doors away—he considered what it must have been like for the mother of the other baby. Was she uncomfortable in the cave? Was she nervous with only her husband there to help her? He chased the thoughts away because he couldn't bear to think of the answers. Creeping at the edge of his consciousness was a wave of shame, held at bay by refusing to give the thoughts any time. He knew the love he felt for his son. He was sure they felt no less for theirs. He hoped their joy was not marred by his selfishness.

Simon understood the awe of birth—the wonder it invoked—but he was still amazed at the talk. Everywhere he went, in hushed tones, people would speculate, looking over their shoulders as they did to keep the talk among faithful Jews. He was intrigued. *They so want their rumors to be true,* he thought, *they seem to give them more credibility by repeating them again and again.*

In the evenings, he would treat himself to thoughts of Alexander and Mara. He, Simon, had a family, a real family! He had never felt so in love with his wife, and each day, he surprised himself with the growing affection he felt for his son.

It took Simon almost a month and a half to make his sales and wind his way back home; but it felt like a year. On the evening he returned, he alternately walked and ran the ten miles up from the seashore. His town was not small, but the Jews huddled in one section of town on the port side, exposing the gate most closely to the path he was on. They mixed comfortably with the Gentiles in the rest of the town, but when it came to homes and traditions, the Jews were most comfortable keeping to themselves. He could see their homes on the horizon as he rushed forward. The young boys and girls playing nearby saw Simon coming and ran for Mara without being asked, to tell her he had returned.

Simon smiled at the gesture and bent over to catch his breath for a few moments. When he straightened up, Mara stood in front of him. She cradled in her arms what could have been mistaken for a bundle of blankets, freshly washed. But from within the folds, a beautiful little pink face looked out with bright eyes. Simon looked down into Alexander's face, and for a moment they were the only three people in the world. He reached up and put his arm around Mara, glancing at her, but returned his gaze to his son while he pulled her close.

"Has he changed?" she asked with a smile.

"Yes, he is so much bigger! But, no, I would know those eyes anywhere. They are your eyes, and I have them emblazoned in my mind."

They both looked at Alexander, then at each other. *Blessed* was the only word he could think of.

That evening, they ate supper together quietly, and then Mara fed Alexander. When she brought the child up to her shoulder to pat his back, Simon said, "It's a beautiful evening. Let's go up to the roof for a little bit."

"Let me bundle him. That would be pleasant."

She wrapped the baby snuggly and began to follow Simon up the stairs. At the top, he stopped suddenly, causing her to bump gently into him.

"Simon, what is it?" she asked.

He said nothing but reached his hand back and held it open for her to hold. She adjusted Alexander in her arms, took Simon's hand, and made the final steps to join him on the roof.

Once there, Mara could see what Simon had glimpsed when he paused at the top of the stairs. On every rooftop, husbands and wives and children stood, silently staring up into the eastern sky.

Simon and Mara followed their gaze to a star on the horizon—a star so bright it lit up their faces and cast shadows around them.

Mara drew close to him. "What is that?" she asked quietly.

Simon just shook his head. "Well, of course, it's a star, but it's new. I have never seen it before, and it's as bright as a full moon."

Something about the situation demanded silence from every onlooker. And so, without a word, Simon and Mara sat on the bench they kept on the roof and just stared. Mara pulled Alexander close to her. Simon noticed and asked, "Does it scare you?"

She looked at him quizzically. "No, it's odd, but not at all frightening. There is something peaceful about it. Look around at our friends. Everyone is curious, but nobody seems concerned."

Because of the bright light, Simon could clearly see the faces of a least six other families. Everyone was mesmerized, but Mara was correct: nobody seemed alarmed.

"Are you frightened?" she asked.

"No, of course not. I just don't know what it is."

"I think I do," she said.

Simon turned to look at her. "You do? How could you know what it is?"

Mara did not answer him directly. Rather, she looked at the star and began speaking: "I shall see him, but not now: I shall behold him, but not nigh: there shall come a Star out of Jacob, and a Scepter shall rise out of Israel . . ."

"You think this has something to do with that baby?" Simon asked incredulously. Mara did not answer. But holding Alexander tightly, she placed her free hand on Simon's arm and nodded.

Simon did not know what to say. He pulled his little family close and continued to stare. *This child*, he thought. *He is but a few months old, and he seems to be changing everything.*

Simon looked down at his own son and tried to chase the thought away. He could almost do it, but his own words, the silent ones in his mind, kept coming back to him: *he seems to be changing everything.*

Although Simon could not really afford do it, he stayed home for nearly two months. The star remained. In fact, it never moved. While other stars arced through the sky, this one held steady. All were amazed, some were unsettled, but even so, after a few weeks, many became used to it and almost ceased to notice it. Simon looked at it every evening but said nothing.

He traded goods in his own village. It never yielded much, but this way he could at least justify staying at home. Every few days he would head down to the port, buy whatever spices were most rare in his community, return to town, and sell them for a meager profit. Everyone knew they could buy the spices cheaper by simply walking down the hill themselves, but this was a small community, and everyone knew everyone else. They laughed amongst themselves at the new father who could not stand to leave his family; and they were willing to pay a few extra shekels to help the family make ends meet.

Finally, the time came when Simon knew he must go on the road again. The evening before he left, Mara and Alexander stayed near his side as he prepared his things, soaking up every chance to be together.

Finally, he finished packing and turned to Mara. "It will go fast."

"You don't believe that, do you," she said. It was not a question but a statement.

He smiled. "No, I don't. But I am trying to tell myself that. I will go as quickly as I can. At least things are peaceful here. You can enjoy your time with Alexander until I return."

The following morning, that peace would be shattered.

9

A commotion outside—originating from somewhere up the street, perhaps—jarred Simon awake. The sleepy new father rubbed his face to become more alert, arose from bed, and dressed hurriedly. Quietly, he opened the door and stepped into the hazy morning air. Uphill from their home was a communal well surrounded by a short stone wall that created a square of sorts. The spot had long been a place for those living nearby to gather and talk. This morning it was filled with many of his friends—all of them listening to a man Simon did not recognize.

Simon quickly approached the square and located his friend Tobias. "What is going on?" he whispered.

"You would not believe it!" Tobias replied. "Actually, what is so terrible is that it *is* believable. But it is so . . . heartbreaking."

"What is?" Simon asked.

"Herod."

Nothing good begins with that name, Simon thought.

His friend continued. "You have heard talk of a baby born in Bethlehem—a baby said to be the fulfillment of prophecy?"

Simon nodded.

"Well, Herod is apparently frightened by this child."

Simon squinted and looked at his friend. "Really? Herod 'the Great'? Troubled by a baby?"

"Not just *any* baby," Tobias said. "This baby is . . ."

"I know, I know," Simon interrupted but then paused. "Wait, so now this baby *is* the prophesied King, not just *possibly* the prophesied King?"

"Well, yes, it is not proven . . ." Tobias said before Simon smiled and interrupted him again.

"It's just that this story gets grander every time I hear it."

He waited for his friend to smile back but became worried when he did not.

"So," Simon rushed on, "I suppose this is not just about Herod being worried, is it?"

Tobias did not answer, so Simon turned his attention to the man addressing the crowd.

"How do you know this?" someone called out.

"The word travels fast. I do not know firsthand, but the man who told me was there and witnessed it."

Another question, spoken with a cracking voice: "How many?"

"I do not know. Some say a dozen, some more." The man paused and became emotional himself. "But if it is even one, it is too many."

Simon was now absorbed and confused. He called out. "I've just gotten here. What's happened?"

Everyone turned to him and started talking at once.

"Shh, shh, shh," Simon said. "I would like to hear it from him."

45

Everyone hushed. The man looked at Simon, winced in visible pain, and began again.

"A baby was born in Bethlehem a little while ago that many believe is the promised child spoken of by Isaiah."

Silence hung thick in the air.

"Some holy men from the East were drawn by the star we have been seeing each night. They went looking for this baby, to honor him. But first they inquired of Herod to learn what he knew. He did not know anything. But the news concerned him. He worried about what the birth of this child would mean to the people. To assure this prophesied King could never be a threat, Herod issued an edict and sent his soldiers to murder every boy born in or near Bethlehem in the last two years." The man paused, took a breath, and simply said, "And they did."

Simon stood frozen, mouth agape. He could not process what he had heard. He had been there—in Bethlehem—not long ago. He had seen babies—many of them. And all of them were now gone? He pictured mothers bent over in anguish, clutching empty clothing, crying uncontrollably. He thought briefly of his son, barely six months old, and his eyes welled with tears.

His mind then turned back to *that* evening. To the cave and its occupants. To the feeling or emotion—or whatever it was—that had drawn the shepherds from their flocks and held them transfixed at the cave's entrance. No matter who the child in that cave was, these murders were a tragedy. But if by some chance the prophecy *was* true and the child in the cave was the future King . . .

He swallowed and called again to the man who had told the

story. "I am sorry, so sorry. Did . . . did you have any family that were . . . lost?"

"No," the man said softly without looking up. "I did not."

Simon spoke again. "Please, one more question. This baby everyone has spoken of so much. Do you know if he is among those taken?"

"I have heard," the man continued, "though not from the same person, that his family was made aware of the danger and fled. I don't know the truth of it, nor have I heard where the family went. These rumors could be untrue but believed by those who hope and pray for his safety. I cannot offer you any confidence about that— only that I heard it and that I pray, like others, that it is true."

As Simon turned to walk back home, he was startled to find Mara in front of him, Alexander clasped tightly in her arms. He could tell she was stifling back tears, holding her lips rigidly to avoid crying out. He walked slowly to her and put both arms around her. Together they looked down at their son, who slept peacefully. Then he felt her shake; she could not hold back any longer. Her soft crying brought on his own, and they stood on the crowded street, weeping for the terrible losses in Bethlehem.

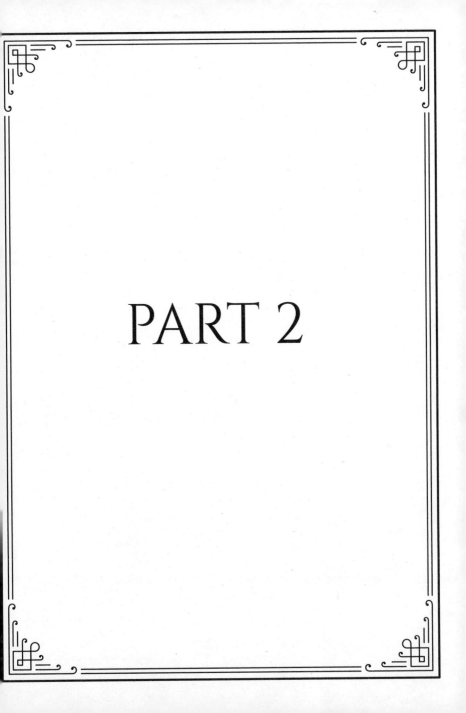

PART 2

10

Despite lingering tales of a king who had been born to save the people, a mysterious new light in the heavens, and a tyrannical ruler who would kill to maintain his throne, life for Simon and Mara went on in quite ordinary ways. Herod's crime against the children was not forgotten by the Jews in the land; but the memory did fade into the fabric of Jewish life under Roman rule.

At first there was much talk of the baby and his family's escape. To Egypt, some said; to the Far East, others said. New details were added to the story with each retelling. Simon believed this tale, like so many before it, would eventually topple from the weight of its incredulity and then be lost to history.

Within a short time, Herod died. The kingdom of Judea was divided between three of his sons, political and geographic boundaries were realigned, and Roman authority continued to press heavily upon the Jews. For Simon, however, all of this was mostly a distraction, something to talk about with other travelers as they shared a meal around the fire after a long day's work. Every now and then, talk of Herod's massacre or of the baby born in Bethlehem would arise. Simon never asked anyone what they knew about the child on these occasions; he simply listened with guarded interest.

And then, one evening, some five or six years after the child's birth, a fellow traveler mentioned the baby. It was out of character for Simon, and he was not sure why he did it, but he asked a question.

"I rarely hear this story about the baby now. It has been years. Do you think the people have stopped believing it?"

The man pushed the embers of the fire with a stick, then looked up and smiled. "No, my friend. And speaking for myself, I absolutely believe it. But I wait. I wait upon this child. I wait upon the Lord."

This both intrigued and troubled Simon. He leaned forward. "Wait . . . for what?"

The man smiled and shook his head. "I am not sure. For whatever the Lord intends—for both this child and for us. I know the boy was not killed. He would be, what, six years old now? That is, perhaps, a little young to lead an army?" He laughed.

Simon smiled. "Yes, of course." He became serious again. "You said you know he was not killed. How do you know that? Have you some firsthand knowledge? Have you seen him?"

The other man looked directly at Simon. "No, I have never seen him, nor his parents. But when I first heard of Herod's act—I can see right where I was, in Bethel, conducting business with a buyer who told me the news. I knew at that moment the child was safe."

Simon leaned forward even farther. "That which you just said. That knowledge. Nobody told you? You did not witness anything. How did you . . . how do you now . . . know that he is safe?"

Simon found the other man's absolutism irritating. These

fanatics were always so sure; everything was always so black and white. Why could they not just say, "As for me, I think . . ."? It was always, "I know . . ." They fairly begged for an argument if you disagreed.

The other man seemed to read Simon's mind, for he approached the question gently albeit firmly. "I understand, my friend. This is hard to comprehend for me too! And it is hard to explain even if one could understand it. All I can say is that something inside of me knows it to be true; I cannot conceive of another way to say it."

"I can help you there," said Simon flippantly. "How about, 'I am not sure'?" He knew it was wrong, but he wanted to get under the skin of this man, to see him flinch when he challenged him. He was disappointed to see the reaction.

Nothing.

"Oh, I understand how to say the sentence. And I know you don't share my belief. But it does not change what I believe."

Simon felt guilty. Why had he done that? It was not like him to prod people with whom he disagreed.

"I'm sorry. I mocked you. I shouldn't have."

"Forgiven," the man said with a smile.

"May we keep speaking of it?"

"Of course."

"This *belief* of yours, this *surety*," Simon continued. "Perhaps you are sure because you so badly want it to be true? Or perhaps because it helps you explain something horrible, like Herod's crime, in a way you can deal with it?"

"You are saying I am lying?"

It was an interesting question. The words seemed an incendiary challenge, but the man's tone was one more of genuine inquiry.

Simon quickly responded. "No, no, I am sorry if it sounds like that. I am suggesting . . . perhaps you have even convinced yourself, so that it is a truth to you?"

The other man looked down with a smile. "I once thought as you do." He stirred the embers for a long time without saying a word. Simon just watched him, sensing he was not done. Finally, still looking into the fire, the man spoke slowly. "I take no offense from your statement, so I hope you will take none from mine. Perhaps it is *you*, not I, that is finding a way to explain something he cannot understand?"

Simon wanted to say he was not offended, but he was. He wanted to lash out, accuse the man of denigrating him by suggesting he could not face uncomfortable facts, to put him in his place and let him know he was out of line. And yet, was this not just exactly what he had said to the man moments before? And here this man was—calm and without guile. Simon looked at the ground and said nothing.

The other man responded to the silence. "I understand. I really do. I am not faulting you. This thing that has happened is unlike anything else we have experienced. It leaves the man who is truly searching speechless."

Simon responded quickly and more sharply than he wished he had. "I am not searching."

Again, the other man was soft and respectful. "This too needs better words. Help me, then, that I might respect you and your beliefs. What is it you are doing by asking me these questions?"

Simon had no answer. He did not know what he was doing. He wanted to ignore everything about this child, to keep his life in order the way he always had. But he could not get away from it. At times he felt the whole thing was an invention of a desperate people who could not face their Roman occupation. What were they clinging to? A baby, born in Bethlehem, whom shepherds left their flocks to see? An unusually bright star?

At other times, he wanted to say he was not sure. But if he said that to those who were discussing it, he knew they would descend on him like flies to honey. They would back him into a corner, pushing him to answer questions that would qualify him as a follower, or not.

If it mattered as much as everyone said, why didn't he believe? If it mattered so little, why could he not clear it from his mind?

All he could think to say was, "More food?"

11

Twelve years after the child was born in Bethlehem, Simon asked Alexander, his firstborn, to join him in his travels.

Like his father before him, Simon had become a master merchant. His travels grew beyond the borders of Judea, Samaria, and Galilee to the more distant regions of the Empire. As his successes increased, so did his family, and he purchased a larger home to accommodate them.

Now when Alexander walked the dusty roads of the Empire with him, he lovingly taught his son the trade: how to identify the best spices, how to negotiate price, which cities brought in the most sales, which roads he should take and which he should avoid, how to recognize people with ill intent and pass them by without drawing attention, and all the nuances of being a merchant.

Simon taught Alexander everything he knew, told him everything he'd learned, shared everything he'd seen in decades of travel. Except one thing. That knowledge he kept to himself. Talk of it did nothing but disrupt the world, his world, and he could see no benefit in sharing that he'd been there on the night this child—this so-called king—was born.

◆　◆　◆

In time, Alexander became a man and married Devorah, a young woman from their village. They lived just a short walk from Simon and Mara. They too had sons.

This is life the way it should be, Simon thought. *Predictable and stable. There is no need to disrupt it.*

He was grateful the stories of the child's birth and the events that followed it were heard only rarely now. At times, months would pass without any mention of them. When something did come up, Simon would find a reason to disengage from the conversation and suggest that he and Alexander move on to another camp. Simon knew that Alexander was aware of the story of the baby. He also knew that Mara held fast to the belief that the child's birth was, indeed, the fulfillment of prophecy. And he knew that Mara often shared her beliefs with their children. He never contradicted her teachings in front of the children, but he did try to balance them by teaching Alexander that when traveler talk turned to speculation about the baby or the prophecy, it was just better to walk away.

Simon told himself he did this because he loved his family. Because it was his duty, to which he was dedicated, to provide stability and predictability. It was a gift he gave those he loved. And it seemed to work.

For a time.

12

Early one spring, in the year Alexander turned thirty, the two of them made another trip to Judea. Simon found current market prices to be so advantageous he purchased four camels in Joppa, rather than the usual donkeys, and acquired as many spices as the animals could carry. Upon arriving in Jerusalem, however, he realized his folly. Nearly every other seller had done the same. As a result, it was nearly impossible to find buyers. He and Alexander tried their luck in some of the surrounding towns but found conditions there to be no different.

After a long and unsuccessful day, the father and son sat in silence around their evening camp fire.

Finally, Simon spoke. "I have been thinking, Alexander. I have an idea."

"Yes?"

"I think we need to get away from Jerusalem. Galilee has always been profitable for us. Why don't we head north?"

"That makes sense."

"But here is my idea. Why don't you take two of the camels and follow the route through Jericho and then up the Jordan River. It may be just far enough away to be different. I will head north and west, sell all I can, and replenish in Caesarea. We will both head to Tiberias and meet there. You remember Levi?"

"Of course, we've stayed in his home many times," Alexander said.

"Whoever gets there first will just wait for the other," Simon said.

They had split up several times before. His son knew the strategy when traveling alone was to find a caravan—of which there were plenty—and stay just ahead of it, always keeping it in sight. He would be far enough away not to get involved but close enough that robbers would be deterred from targeting a single man walking.

"That sounds fine," Alexander said. "One condition, however . . ."

"What is that?"

"You take that older one. That animal has a desire to hurt me. Whoever sold you that one must still be laughing."

His father smiled. "Done."

He then continued. "I would think, perhaps, three or four weeks?"

"I'll miss your company, but I will take advantage of the solitude."

In the morning, the two men rose well before dawn to get as many cool hours on the road as they could. Simon put his arms around his son and hugged him. "God be with you until we meet in Galilee."

His son smiled and returned the hug. "You know, I have a feeling he will. And God be with you."

Something about the way Alexander said it caught Simon's attention. He did not know why, so he pushed it out of his mind.

With that, the two men, each with two camels in tow, parted ways.

13

Simon's journey west led him through Emmaus and Lydda to Joppa, where he refreshed his goods and turned north, traveling up the coastal Roman highway to Caesarea. In Caesarea, he restocked once more and again continued northward, toward the hilly terrain of Mount Carmel. Eventually he turned inland, crossing the Plain of Esdraelon and arriving in the mountainous region south of Mount Tabor. There, he spent several days visiting towns in the area and quickly ran through his supply of wares. His hunch had been right: outside the vicinity of Jerusalem, sales were much better. So much so that instead of heading straight through Galilee to Tiberias, he decided he would return to the coast and replenish his stores before reuniting with Alexander.

His plan was to walk northwest to Ptolemais, a busy city on the Phoenician coast. The port there was well developed and provided easy landing for the numerous large trading ships arriving daily. In Ptolemais, Simon knew he would find a vast selection of goods. His plan was to empty his bags—by selling through his current supply of spices—in the Galilean villages he passed along the way. He would visit as many of these small towns as possible, avoiding only one: Nazareth.

The most obvious reason for this decision was that of all the towns along the route, Nazareth was quite possibly the smallest and was, therefore, not likely to elicit many sales. But Simon had an additional motive for avoiding the village. During his travels of the past few years, he had heard talk—unsubstantiated talk, he told himself—that the child born three decades earlier in Bethlehem was now the man called Jesus who lived in Nazareth. Simon had no desire to find himself near the epicenter of such rumors, especially if there would be no economic advantage reached by stopping there.

❖ ❖ ❖

His plan worked out exactly as he'd hoped: his bags were empty when he arrived in Ptolemais, and he was able purchase enough new goods to stuff them to their seams before leaving for Tiberias. His route east, back through Galilee, would not include any stops, for he hoped to reach Levi's home as soon as possible. He was anxious to see Alexander again.

A few days later, when Simon arrived at his old friend's home, Alexander was there waiting for him.

"Father!" Alexander exclaimed as he saw him. He swung his arms around him exuberantly.

"Hello, son. I see you have made it safely. Did all go well?"

"More than well, Father," he said almost anxiously. "It all went so well! Beyond my hopes. I have so much to tell you."

His father chuckled. One of the little pleasures of this vocation was sharing stories of the road—dangers encountered along the way, strange and exotic people met in different lands, transactions of an unusually successful nature.

The table was already set for dinner, however, and so the stories would have to wait. Levi and his family joined Simon and Alexander for the meal. As the group ate, they talked of the goings-on in the region. Occasionally, however, Simon noticed that one or another of the individuals at the table would pause, as if he wanted to mention something new but was afraid to share it. A moment of awkward silence would ensue, and then the conversation would pick back up.

When they finished eating, Simon said to Levi, "If it's all right with you, my son and I will go to your roof and catch up on each other's lives since we parted."

"Of course," his friend said with a tone that made Simon almost curious. Simon saw Levi and his wife exchange a quick glance but shrugged it off in his rush to visit with Alexander.

Once up on the roof, Simon was eager to hear more about the unusual experiences Alexander had hinted at. "Tell me, did you find success?"

"I did," Alexander said. "My bags were empty when I arrived! Those cities along the Jordan get so few visits from traveling merchants that there was no problem with demand, or price. All went very well."

Simon sensed that his son was holding something back, but he didn't broach the subject.

"I think, perhaps, my son has surpassed me," he said instead. "I am proud of you."

"Thank you, Father. And you?"

"Things also went well for me. I replenished three times, which is why I took so long getting here. I found the same thing. Once out of Jerusalem, prices were quite acceptable. I suppose we needn't have split up."

Alexander took a breath, then replied, "I am glad we did."

Simon was a bit surprised. "Tired of me?" he asked jokingly.

His son enthusiastically looked at him. "Father, something happened on this journey. I have been so anxious to tell you about it."

"Is that why everyone kept looking at each other so strangely at dinner? I don't think Levi and Avigail have shared that many intense glances since they were newly betrothed."

"Yes," his son smiled. "This is controversial, and it's dividing people. I think they were not sure how you would react."

"Well, now you have my attention. Go ahead."

His son leaned toward him, "Father, when I passed through Jericho, there were many people on the road, all heading the same direction. We began talking. They had just come from an oasis there in the wilderness outside the city. Do you know this man they call Jesus?"

Simon feigned ignorance. "Is this the man some claim is the prophesied one come to save us from the Romans?"

His son sat back. "Father, I'm surprised. I did not know you paid attention to these stories. Yes, this is the one. You know of him?"

"I have heard his name. Was he there at this oasis?"

"He was! There was also a man there they call John the Baptist. They say he lives a spartan life in the wilderness, though he comes from a line of priests. He teaches people principles that he says were given to him directly from God."

"Is he an expert in the law?" his father interrupted.

"No, that is what is so interesting. He . . ."

"Then if he is not, why listen to his claims that God is talking to him? Isn't that sacrilege?"

"Perhaps if he was not hearing from God. But, Father, I think he truly is."

There was silence between the men for a long period. Finally, Simon asked quietly, "What makes you think so?"

"It is hard to explain. When I heard what he taught, something inside me whispered it was truth. He speaks of care for the poor. If you have two coats, and another has none, he says, you should give one to him. He told the publicans they should be exact in their taxing and take no more than appropriate. And to the soldiers he said, 'Do violence to no man.'"

"But these things," Simon replied, "are not new things. We have always been kind to the poor. We have all complained about the publicans and their taxes. And to tell the soldiers not to do violence? Isn't that like telling our donkeys not to bray?"

"Perhaps, but he is saying it out loud. We have said those things in hushed tones to one another but never to the publicans and soldiers. He speaks to them directly, confidently, in public." Then, speaking more carefully, Alexander went on. "And, Father, we've seen many without a coat, when we have had plenty. But have we always shared what we could?"

Simon became defensive. "Alexander, we have always been generous. You know we have offered food and more to those we passed who seemed to be in need. But they have to deserve it. I will not hand something to a beggar who refuses to work or to try to improve his own condition."

Alexander fell silent. Finally he asked, "And who decides if they deserve it, Father?"

"I do! As you need to. Alexander, you will quickly have nothing if you give to everyone who asks. Does this Jesus person also suggest that? How does one live in the world that way?"

Simon was becoming agitated, so Alexander tried to calm him down.

"Your point is right, Father. I don't understand all of this—it's new to me too. All I know is that I did not hear 'Give him your coat if you think he deserves it.'"

Simon looked away. He was a devoted father. He had not only taught his children good values but had shown them the way to survive in a world that would not seek to serve them. He felt misjudged.

Alexander trod carefully. "Father, I didn't mean to offend you. You've taught me well, and I recognize this. But these teachings are both interesting and confusing to me. It would help me if I could tell you more without you getting angry."

Simon looked back and nodded. Despite the internal struggle he felt, he wanted to support Alexander.

"There is so much more. He warns them that if they do not repent of these things, they will suffer before God. Yet, at the same time, he tells them they *can* repent and that God is willing, *anxious*, to forgive them."

"And does anyone listen to this?" Simon asked.

"Many do. John says that if they wish to be forgiven, they need to be baptized, and they line up in droves to be baptized by him."

"But," Simon protested, "who is this John? How does he claim authority to do this? He speaks more broadly than our leaders in the synagogue, but he has no authorization?"

"Well, this is one of the amazing parts. He claims authority, but not from any man." Again, Alexander paused. "He says he was called directly by God."

"So he is called to command us to repent because we can't take care of ourselves?"

"No, it's not that. It's that what he teaches is different. This kindness to others, this honesty. And, yes, he warns us that if we do not honor these things, we will suffer God's wrath."

His father stood and looked out at the horizon.

"Son, I don't know what to tell you. You heard someone tell you this—you did not even hear it from the man himself. But you claim to *know* that this John hears directly from God because you just . . . *know* it?" Simon paused. "Well, I am now hearing *you* tell me the same things, and I feel none of it. Why is that, if what you say is true?"

"I don't know. But there is still more."

His father sat back down and looked at him. "Oh yes," he said, "we still need to bring Jesus into the story, don't we?"

It wasn't really a question. It was a statement. A derogatory one.

Alexander ignored him. "These people I walked with, they said that John has been preaching for a few years, and he has said multiple times that his mission is to prepare the way. He is to prepare the way for one he calls 'the Lamb of God.' He said that this man will take away the sins of the world. He also said that when the man was ready, he would come to John to be baptized. Well, while they were there, this man *did* come, and it was Jesus. John knew he was the one—the Lamb of God—as soon as he saw him, and he called him the Son of God. Jesus asked John to baptize him, and John said he was not worthy; it was he who needed to be baptized by Jesus. But Jesus insisted."

Simon just stared at his son.

"And, Father, this is the most amazing part. John told others that when he baptized Jesus, the Spirit of God came upon Jesus in the form of a dove."

"Form of a dove? What does that mean?"

"I am not sure, but they said John attested to it. And he heard a real, tangible voice from heaven say, 'This is my Beloved Son.'"

Simon sat quietly for a while before asking, "And you believe all of this?"

Alexander stood and walked closer to his father, who had sat on a bench by the edge of the roof and was looking away from his son. The younger man knelt, took his father gently by the shoulder, and turned him so they were looking at each other eye to eye. "I do. I think he speaks the truth. I cannot tell you how I know exactly, but I just know. I believe all of it. Every word."

"And, son, you know I love you. But what if I told you I think you are foolish and being deceived?"

Simon felt a little guilty as the question slipped out of his mouth. Alexander was a great man, Simon knew, but he was also known to have a fiery temper on occasion. And because his son's absolutism about the topic infuriated him so much, he had asked the question with the intention of provoking that temper.

The fiery passion, however, did not make an appearance.

Alexander's reply was calm and measured. "Father, I would not be offended. I wish you did not think that, but I respect your right to think differently. Most importantly, it will not change what I believe."

Simon's memory took him back twenty-five years, to a time when he was about Alexander's age. He was sharing a fire with a fellow traveler and, in like fashion, had tried to provoke the traveler. But the traveler, in a fashion almost exactly like Alexander's just now, had replied, "I know you don't share my belief. But it does not change what I believe."

For a moment, or perhaps for less than a moment, something happened. It was as if one had lit a candle in the wind. The flame had gone out quickly, but then some errant spark had brought it back to life, reigniting and brightening it.

Suddenly, Simon was not annoyed. He was curious. No, he was desirous. He *needed* to know what it was that made the traveler all those years ago, and Alexander this very night, say almost the same thing about the same Jesus. Furthermore, there was a deep craving inside Simon to believe in something so surely and completely.

But there was a second emotion that came quickly after the first: fear. Something scared Simon about the idea of believing so strongly, of *knowing for certain*. There was a comfort in ambiguity. But this, this was foreign—a feeling without precedent for him.

He did not know what to do with it, and so he separated himself from it.

He snickered.

And with that, all of the insights that had coursed through his brain were gone as quickly as they had come. He felt shallow and empty.

"Well, you believe what you believe, and I will believe what I believe," he said.

"That's fine," Alexander answered calmly. "But, Father, I ask you: What is it that you *do* believe? You know the prophecies. Do you not believe them? Or do you believe in them but just don't believe this is time for them to be fulfilled?"

"I think it's the latter. I believe them, but this is not it."

"Well," his son replied. "That's bold. Do you have evidence? Why are you so sure? Why do you *know* Jesus is not the one in the prophecy?"

Simon laughed defensively and waved a finger at Alexander. "You won't draw me in with that. Challenging me because I *feel* I am right? Clever!"

Alexander was not amused. But neither was he angry.

"This is not a trick, Father. It's a real question. If you don't believe it, is it because you believe something else? And if so, what is it that you believe? And why?"

Then, with just a spark of his temper shining through, Alexander added, "And why is your belief any more valid than mine?"

This has become less about learning and more about sparring, Simon thought in exasperation.

"Look, Alexander, I don't know. I just don't think this man Jesus, good as he may be, is the promised one."

"Father, don't you understand? I respect your right to think that. I'm just asking you to give me one reason you believe that."

Simon was silent, and angry. All had been so good in his family. Just weeks ago, he and Alexander had been enjoying their time together on the road. He was satisfied with his life, his marriage, and his children. Why did this Jesus person have to disrupt everything? And why couldn't he, Simon, get away from it? No matter where he turned, there was always someone talking about it. And now it had found its way into his own family.

Simon stood near the edge of the roof, pretending to admire the sunset. And though Alexander remained by his side, his gaze also fixed on the setting sun, Simon could feel the emotional distance growing rapidly between them.

14

All night, Simon thought about his discussion with Alexander—or was it an argument? He was perplexed. Why was his son so moved by these stories when he, Simon, felt only confusion? As he dissected their conversation, he realized that he was not mad at his son; he was uncomfortable. This was his first child! He knew this boy well. It had been nearly two decades since Alexander began traveling with his father, learning the trade, working side by side day in and day out. They had rarely gone more than a few days without seeing each other. Simon knew Alexander's great strengths; and there were so many. He also knew his weaknesses; and there were so few. Just days ago, if he had been asked to guess his son's reaction to these tales, he would have answered without hesitation that Alexander's feelings matched his own.

It scared him to know he was wrong. But he couldn't figure out *why* it scared him.

His son *did* seem different, but in only good ways. He had remained patient when Simon intentionally pushed his patience. There was a feeling of peace about him. He was calm—confident, even.

However, the most prominent thought that kept coming to his

mind was the question Alexander had asked him. "But, Father, I ask you: What is it that you *do* believe?"

Simon suddenly realized with incredible distress that he did not know. He could recite some of what he had heard his whole life, but this question was deeper. What was it he actually believed? This frightened him. How had he had lived more than fifty years and not truly pondered and answered this question?

He tossed and turned as his son's question repeated itself over and over again in his mind.

Finally, as the night sky began to lighten, Simon gave up on sleep. Levi's home was large and had afforded both he and his son separate rooms. He crept quietly to where Alexander was sleeping to wake him. They planned to travel north today, toward Capernaum, and would need to get an early start so they could supply the merchants along the way before the daily markets opened.

Simon also knew that getting back to a routine on the road would relieve some of the tension between them. He peered into the room where Alexander was staying and was just about to speak when he realized the room was empty.

Rather than worry, Simon felt a sense of pride swell within him. The empty room meant that Alexander must already be up, likely preparing their animals and goods for the day's travels. *What discipline! Another one of Alexander's many strengths,* he thought as he exited the house. He walked around back, pleased with how well the day was starting out, and found his son just finishing up.

"Well done!"

"Thank you, Father. I wanted to be able to help you get ready to leave the best I could."

Simon stopped and looked at his son. "Help *me*? Aren't *we* going to Capernaum?"

His son looked down at the ground for a moment before raising his head to meet his father's eyes. "No, Father, I am not going . . ."

"Alexander!" Simon exclaimed. "If this is about last night, I was tired, and I am sure . . ."

"No," he said quietly. "This has got nothing to do with last night. I would have told you then had things not become so tense. I had already decided not to go with you."

"And when did these plans change?"

Alexander did not answer that question but instead addressed the one he knew his father really wanted to ask. "Jesus is here. He has returned from Jericho, and he is teaching the people. I want to hear him, to understand more of what he is saying."

Simon was not surprised. One of the many concerns he had turned over in his mind during the night was that this would happen. He had hoped they were just the churnings of fear that always seemed to accompany sleepless nights. Clearly they were not.

"Alexander, I understand. Well, no, I do not understand, but I know it is important to you. But is it more important than . . ."

"It is, Father. It's that important."

"You don't know what I was going to say."

"I don't need to. Whatever you compare it to, this is more important."

His son then softened his tone a little, and his eyes changed from determination to compassion. "Father, you know how much I love you, and you know I would never try to hurt you. I worried that telling you this would hurt you, so if you understand nothing else—though I wish you would—understand this: This is so important that I risk hurting you to do it."

"So important to *you,* you mean?"

"No! So important. Period. It is important to everyone, and to you."

Simon said nothing else. He walked around Alexander and finished the job of packing the animals. Without looking at his son, he asked flatly, "Will you be keeping any of the spices to sell, or should I take them all?"

"If it's all right with you, I will take just one camel's worth. That will give me enough to make my way home."

Simon nodded, again without looking. He then continued working for a moment before saying, "Pick the one you would like and load up what you want."

"Well, one thing I know is I'm not taking that one," Alexander said, trying to lighten the mood as he pointed to the older animal he had shunned earlier in their travels. Simon remembered the reference but forced himself not to smile. That carefree relationship with his son was a lifetime ago. It was gone now. Simon was determined not to show any friendliness. Alexander could tell, and if he was at first offended, he now appeared only to be frustrated.

They finished packing while also avoiding standing next to each other to minimize the awkwardness of the silence. When he was ready, Simon pulled on his lead camel, which prompted the others to follow. He walked to the gate, then stopped. Turning halfway so that his son could just see his profile, he spoke one more time. "Do you know when you will make your way home?"

"I don't, Father. But I will not be long behind you. Please tell Devorah."

Simon nodded once more and began to walk again.

His son called out, "Shalom, Father. God keep you and be with you until we meet again."

Simon did not reply. He tried to hide the weariness of his step and the heaviness of his heart as he walked down the road and turned out of sight.

15

Simon found the remainder of his trip to be profitable, but he took little joy in it.

As he worked his way through the towns and villages along the road to the coast, he was continually met with throngs of people heading in the direction from which he'd come. The groups were never as large as those he encountered during Passover season; but they were still quite significant. More people on the roads meant more people frequenting the markets along the way. And this, of course, meant there were more merchants in need of his goods. Although it would keep him from getting home as quickly as he'd hoped, Simon decided to take advantage of the situation. After all, at least while trading, he was able to get Alexander off his mind. *Jesus has certainly done one thing for me,* he thought to himself. *He is drawing crowds.*

As Simon worked, he continued to divide his earnings, saving half for Alexander. He tried to convince himself it was out of caring for his son, but deep inside, he knew it was a feeble attempt to bring comfort to himself, to preserve things the way they had been.

Eventually he found his way to Ptolemais, where he planned

to secure passage on a ship that would carry him across the Mediterranean and back home to Mara. Sometimes he traveled on Jewish ships, which he preferred. But Roman-captained vessels came and went more frequently, so he often found himself traveling with people he'd rather avoid. He knew, though, that if he laid low, it was unlikely that anyone would speak to him on the journey.

On this occasion, he had timed his sales well, trading the last of his goods a day before arriving in the port city. He had then sold his travel bags and his camels to incoming traders looking to do exactly what Simon had just done. And so, today, as he waited at the port, he was left with only his money, hidden carefully beneath his garments.

He found a place to sit on the wall by the sea, where he could watch for incoming ships. If he was not picky about the travel accommodations, he knew he'd be able to find a ship headed in the right direction in a matter of hours. But it was early still, and the winds were light, so there were no ships in sight at present. He sat back and let the sun play on his face. *Ah*, he thought, *something familiar*.

As he relaxed, he looked around, surveying the water that shimmered in the morning sunlight and watching the last of the fishermen head out with their nets. He enjoyed being in busy port towns, where a variety of people from all over the world worked and lived together. He turned his head one way and then the other to loosen his neck. On that second turn, he found himself gazing up at Mount Carmel, a few miles distant. He paused, then turned his body to fully face it.

Mount Carmel held a special fascination for him. One of the few scripture stories he remembered hearing in his youth was that of the prophet Elijah challenging the priests of Baal, which had occurred right there on the slopes of Mount Carmel generations and generations ago. The people of Ahab had trespassed the commandments of God. Elijah was repulsed by their wickedness and by the depravity of the priests, who spent their days succumbing to an idol god. He directed Ahab to gather all of Israel to the mount. There, Elijah forced them to confront their indecision, saying, "If the Lord is your God, follow him. But if Baal, then follow him."

He called for two young bulls to be brought forth as a sacrifice. He gave one bull to the priests of Baal and told them to prepare it for slaughter upon the altar. But rather than light a fire in the conventional fashion, they were to call on their god to send down a flame to ignite the wood and burn the sacrifice. He would keep the other bull and do the same on a separate altar. Whichever god answered with fire, he proclaimed to the people, would be the one, true God.

The wicked priests prepared their bull and began calling on Baal to ignite the sacrifice. From morning until noon, they yelled, "Oh, Baal, hear us." But no fire came down. Elijah mocked the priests, suggesting that their god must be talking to someone else, or perhaps he was on a journey, or maybe he was asleep and they needed to wake him. They continued pleading to Baal, cutting themselves and crying out, to no avail.

When it came time for the evening sacrifice, Elijah built a second altar, laying out twelve stones for the base to signify the twelve tribes of Israel and building a wooden platform to set atop the stones. He dressed his bull and placed it upon the altar. And then he dug a trench around the altar.

He asked the people to collect four barrels, each filled to the brim with water, then directed them to pour the water over the altar. They were made to repeat the task twice more. Finally, he filled the trench surrounding the altar with water. And then Elijah called boldly out to his God: "Hear me, O Lord, hear me, that this people may know that thou art the Lord God, and that thou hast turned their heart back again."

God heard Elijah. Almost immediately, fire came down from the heavens, so much fire that the flames burnt the sacrifice, the wood, the stones, and the dust round about it. Not a drop of water remained in the trench. Those watching fell upon their faces and proclaimed Elijah's God the Lord.

Simon loved this story because he admired Elijah's conviction and certainty. However, it meant even more to him because his wise father, after telling the story, would compare Simon to Elijah. He would pull him close and tell him he was strong like Elijah, that he had seen Simon make difficult, correct decisions. As an adult, looking back, Simon realized that this was his father's way of letting his son know he was always watching, always ready to build him up and support him. Whenever his father would retell the story and liken Simon to Elijah, he would always finish with a warning: "My son, never permit yourself to be double-minded like the people of Ahab. Choose one way or another and live by it. A man who lives in the space between his choices is of no use to anyone."

Simon committed to his father's challenge every time.

Suddenly, in this quiet moment beneath the shadows of Mount Carmel, Simon felt like a bystander watching his own life and actions play out in front of him. When he thought of the last few months, in particular, a question permeated his mind.

"What has happened to me?"

But then, just as quickly as the moment had come, it was gone—though not without leaving an echo of sadness in him. His attention was drawn to the docks, where a ship had put in. Several men leapt off and were unloading baskets of grain. Simon walked up and caught the attention of the captain, rapidly securing passage.

16

Within an hour, the ship was again at sea.

Simon was somewhat pleased with how it had worked out. The ship was typical, about fifty feet long, which provided room for him to sit in relative quiet and minimize his interaction with the Roman captain. Roman sailors were tough men and known to challenge the Jews they took on as passengers for no apparent reason other than sport. Simon paid full price for his passage, and as such, was not given any responsibilities. The winds were at their back. With two stops between Ptolemais and his home port, he would be only four or five days on the water. After that, it was an easy half day's walk up into the hills to his family.

During the first afternoon, as Simon was sitting and reflecting on his journey, the captain came to his side.

"May I join you?"

That was an unusual question. A captain never needed permission to be anywhere on board his own ship. Simon prepared himself for a prodding.

"Of course," Simon replied cautiously.

The man sat next to Simon on a grate that covered the opening to the storage holds below. Simon looked toward the stern at the raised deck, where a young boy was controlling the rudder. Without following his gaze, the captain said, "Don't worry. He's my son. The last of six. He's fourteen but has been sailing with me for several years. He knows this ship as well as I do. When we run with a steady wind like this, I give him a chance to pilot the ship. You're safe."

The captain was unusually friendly. Simon smiled and opened up. "I wasn't worried. My sons have worked with me as well. I trust an earnest young man's ability if his father has set a good example." He then felt a wave of melancholy come over him, and he thought of Alexander, how their relationship had been and how it seemed to be now. He needed to think of something different.

"You are Roman?" Simon asked.

The captain smiled and waved his hand slowly around him. "You see my ship. It is Roman, is it not? Her markings are Roman. There is Roman grain below, and we are sailing the perimeter of the Roman Empire. Does not seem to leave much question, does it?"

The answer seemed deliberately vague, which intrigued Simon, so he emboldened himself and replied, "Yes. All these things *are* Roman. But I asked if you were."

The captain smiled again. "I . . . live in Portus, twenty miles from Rome. If that makes me a Roman, I suppose I am."

"Then I will leave it there."

"It's fine," the captain replied. "I have nothing to hide. I suppose I just have a difficult time saying I am Roman. I enjoy many benefits of being part of Rome, but I am troubled by so much of what is done in the name of Rome that I refuse to hand them my identity."

They were quiet for a minute, and the captain said, "So, you seem to find a great deal to look at as we sail. Is this your first time at sea?"

"Oh, no," Simon replied. "I don't think I could count the times I've been on these waters. I'm a merchant. I have been doing this for forty years." He paused. "This particular trip has given me a lot to think about, and I suppose I am lost in my thoughts."

"Your trade suffers?"

"No, not that. In fact, this may have been my best trip ever."

"Excuse me for saying more than I should, but you don't look like a man who may have just had his best trip ever, so I will leave you to your thoughts."

"Actually," Simon said, "it is good to talk to someone. If your son is still handling things to your satisfaction, I'd like to ask you a question."

The captain did not look back at his son. Instead, he surveyed the sails, the water, and the direction of this ship before saying, "He's fine. Go ahead."

"Have you heard of this person, Jesus, from Nazareth?"

The captain's demeanor suddenly shifted, and he seemed cautious. "Why?"

"You have, then? It seems to concern you that I asked."

Without hesitating, the captain replied. "Again, why do *you* ask?"

"My son, my eldest, began this journey with me. We have worked together for eighteen years now. We split up during our journey, and then met again a month later in Tiberias. While he was alone, he ran into people who were coming from the baptism of this Jesus by some wild man named John out in the wilderness by Jericho."

The captain watched Simon carefully but said nothing.

"When I saw him again, he was full of . . ." Simon was not sure what to call it. "Full of . . . zeal for what the people had shared about John's and about Jesus's teachings."

The captain finally spoke. "This son of yours, this is the one you thought of when you referred to an earnest young man?"

"It is."

"So, then, if this earnest man who was once an earnest *young* man is enthused about the teachings of these two, what do you think of that?"

Now Simon was cautious. "I am sorry, but why do you ask?"

"You brought it up. You seem troubled."

Simon trusted this man for some reason, so he decided to continue. "I am a Jew . . ."

The captain cut him off. "As am I."

Simon seemed surprised, and it was not lost on the captain. "There are a great number of us in Rome. We have been there for centuries. My ancestors were brought from Greece as slaves and eventually purchased their freedom."

Simon was relieved. "Then you will understand. Jesus is not a scribe, but he claims authority directly from God. My son is so mesmerized by him he has stayed behind to hear more. I am afraid for him."

The captain looked at him. "Afraid in what way? What do you fear he will do?"

Simon paused. "Follow him, I suppose."

"And, if he does, what will become of that?"

"I don't know. Leave our business? Leave his family?"

"Well, that would upset me if it happened to my son. What is it that this Jesus teaches that may cause him to do that?"

Simon could tell these questions were not entirely genuine. This man knew more than he was letting on. However, it was helping him think things through, so he continued.

"I don't know that much, but he did share these thoughts . . . let me remember how he put it . . . If you have two coats and another has none, give him one of yours."

The captain frowned mockingly. "Oh, I see your concern now, how that could lead to leaving his family."

Simon was not amused. "He said they spoke of the publicans being more honest in levying taxes, and the soldier not exacting violence upon any man."

The captain put his hands in the air. "Our world is coming apart!" he yelled. The crew members looked his way to see if he was all right. "What would we do with honest publicans and peaceful soldiers? There would then be nothing to complain about, as we would all be warm with our shared coats."

This annoyed Simon, and he stopped. The captain slapped him on his back and chuckled. "I am sorry, I didn't mean to offend you. It just doesn't sound that tragic."

Simon then continued. "All right, then. What about John claiming he was called by God to prepare the way for Jesus? And, even more, what about Jesus claiming he is the Son of God? Does that bother you?"

Before the captain could answer, Simon looked at him. "My assumption is you have heard these points as well?"

"I have. I concede it's a little harder to believe John's calling. And, to accept that Jesus is the Son of God, I have to admit I had to think about it."

"That's what I mean," said Simon. "It's troubling."

The captain did not respond to Simon's last comments but continued with what he was saying. "However, I did think about it. And when I did, I felt, for some reason, that he was telling the truth."

Simon turned and faced him directly. "So you know all about this. You have heard these things?"

"I have. I am in and out of the ports all along the eastern shores many times a year. I have recently carried passengers going to Galilee in curiosity and returning practically on fire, like your son. On our long trips in the quiet out here, I have asked them about it, and it makes sense to me inside. It is different than I was brought up on, but to be honest, I have been often troubled by what I was brought up on. I have always cared about others—it's my nature. When I hear of some of the harshness preached by the priests, it doesn't sit well with me. But when I hear the teachings of Jesus, I hear what I already believe, and it seems not just to be good admonition but how we are supposed to be—how God wants us to be."

Simon turned back to face the side of the ship. He leaned over, elbows on his knees, hands clasped, and hung his head. Almost imperceptibly, he said, "I cannot make sense of all of this."

The captain sat quietly for a short time, staring out at the shoreline. Finally, he took a breath, as though he had just come up with something. "Let me tell you this. I have become a follower of this man, but there is a great deal I don't understand. I know only what I have heard from those who have heard from someone else. But this is something I am going to pursue learning more about. Your journey is your business, and I cannot tell you what to think or do. But I only ask you this: If your son, because of following Jesus, is kinder to the poor, is more honest, is more caring, is that a bad thing?"

"But," Simon protested, "he is already those things!"

"Then perhaps he, like me, has heard affirmation of what he already believes." The captain put his hand on Simon's shoulder. "No doubt from a father who is a good example."

Simon caught his breath, stifling the emotion that overcame him with that statement.

"My friend," the captain continued, "it is my opinion that if it is true that this man is the Son of God, the one prophesied, then you cannot afford *not* to follow him, which means you need to give his words a chance to grow within you."

In the back of his mind, Simon heard Elijah challenging the Israelites to choose. The captain said nothing else but stood and left, resuming his position at the helm of his ship.

17

The remaining days on board ship were uneventful. They took on more passengers at the next stop, so Simon and the captain didn't have the chance to reconnect in private. However, just as Simon was about to go ashore at his destination, the captain called out for him to join him.

"My friend, I have been thinking about you, and I have been praying for you, and a thought has come to me. May I share it?"

"Of course," Simon said warmly. He liked this man, his honesty and humility especially.

"My thought is this: If you believe what the holy scriptures say—that a Messiah will come—then you must also believe that the Messiah will change our lives. And if so many others believe this Jesus is the Messiah, isn't it worth your time to investigate?"

Simon paused for a moment and looked up and down the shoreline as he thought about it. "Let's say I believe the scriptures," he began. "Am I not, then, already investigating? I have listened to my son. I am listening to you."

"I suppose in a way," the captain said. "But you are letting it come to you. Should you not seek it out?"

Before Simon could respond, the captain went on. "Not long

ago, one of my passengers heard Jesus speak in person and shared with me many of the things Jesus taught. A frequent teaching was to 'seek the kingdom of God.' I don't think that means waiting for old, slightly addled men like me to come find you." The captain smiled.

Simon looked around to be sure he had privacy from the crew as they unloaded the ship. "Then tell me," he said in a hushed tone. "How? I want to seek. But I don't know what to do."

He looked pleadingly at the captain, and the captain gestured for them to move to the side of the ship, where they could lean against the rail as they talked.

"Listen, as I have said, I am just learning myself. But I had the same question. One of my passengers and I discussed it, and he said Jesus had spoken to this very thing, that he had taught *how* one should seek."

Simon looked intently at him, and the sounds of the crew around them seemed to fade away, as if they were being muted or blocked somehow.

"There are three things Jesus says one should do," the captain said. "The first is to ask." He pointed to the sky.

Simon looked up, puzzled.

The captain chuckled and pointed up again. "*He* has all the answers, all of them, every single one. Ask him for what you wish."

Simon did not move.

"This man told me that Jesus promised if you ask, it will be given to you what you are asking. Not maybe, not partially. Just simply, 'It shall be given you.'"

The captain folded his arms as he leaned against the gunwale, looking out to sea. "So many times, I have been out on these waters when they've become angry and wanted me in their depths. There have been dark nights and massive waves. I've felt totally lost. And what did I do? What you or anyone would do. I asked God to help me. I asked him to keep me safe."

Simon hung on every word. "And did he?"

The captain looked at him for a moment and then burst out laughing. Simon was confused but then felt sheepish as the captain spread his arms wide. "Well, here is the proof."

"Of course, I know you were kept alive. But did he always protect you perfectly?"

"Ahh, that, my friend, is a very good question. I suppose it depends on what you mean by 'perfectly.' Was I never injured? Was my boat never damaged? No, both these things have happened. I have broken limbs, I have had to repair my ship. Other times, I have arrived at shore without harm. But! Each time I was safe, as I had asked for."

"When you *were* hurt," Simon proceeded, "do you think it was because you did not ask as well as another time? Why would he answer you differently when your request was always the same?"

The captain shook his head. "I suppose I always could do better, but I don't think that's it. I think he answered me in the way I needed to be answered at the time. When I was not harmed, I was grateful. When I was harmed, I found I learned something that helped me be safer after that. Experience has taught me that I should be patient, should wait upon the Lord and see what he has in store for me."

Simon sighed in exasperation. "Seek. Ask. You tell me I should do these things. You say he will answer any questions. Then, in the next sentence, you say I should wait and be patient when he *doesn't* answer. Which is it?"

The captain thought for a moment. "You said you have a son. May I ask his name?"

"Three sons, actually, but the one I referred to is my oldest, Alexander."

"When Alexander was young, did you require him to help you with tasks the family needed done?"

"Of course, always."

"Very good. And did he ever complain?"

Simon laughed. "Always as well—at least when he was young. And particularly when we cleaned the stables."

The captain shook his finger. "Very good. And I suppose, when he did complain, you did not give in and let him stop working?"

"No, never."

"But couldn't you have done his work in half the time yourself? And were he to give up anyway and not finish, would the sun not have risen the next morning?"

"Yes, I could have. And I am sure the sun would have been fine. But he needed to learn to work hard, to be responsible, to follow through."

"And *did* he learn those things?"

Simon paused for a moment and then quietly answered, "Remarkably so. He does everything with such commitment. If you need to count on someone, he is the best you will ever meet."

The captain waited a moment to let that thought settle in—for both of them. "So I suppose the young Alexander needed to wait, to suffer a little—at least in his mind—to be patient as you taught him, so that he might gain the greater gift of responsibility. You knew that. And you let him wait until he learned for himself."

Simon shook his head and smiled. "I first heard that phrase 'Wait upon the Lord' many years ago, but this is the first time it has made sense to me."

Both men looked out to sea, watching the sun's rays glimmer off the water.

"Oh," Simon said. "There were three things. That is one. What are the other two?"

The captain smiled. "The first was ask, as we said. The second, is to seek, as you are doing right now. Look for answers. The Lord speaks in many different voices and in many different ways. Words, memories, examples, through others, and more. And, like asking, he said if you seek, you *will* find."

"And the last?"

The captain became more serious. "This last one strikes me as most profound. I have pondered it a great deal, and if it makes sense to you, I would encourage you to learn more about it than I can tell you. The last is 'Knock, and it shall be opened unto you.'"

"Knock, as in on a door?"

"I believe that is what it means."

They both stood in silence once again, until finally the captain nodded toward his busy crew and said, "Well, I am not a passenger. I need to get to work."

Simon clasped the captain's hand and shook it firmly. "Thank you. You've been helpful to me—" He hesitated momentarily. "One more question, if I may. Why is it that you, and all these followers of this man, seem to want to engage anyone you can in a conversation about him? Has he ordered you to do so?"

"No." The captain chuckled. "I believe it is this. When you find something that brings you this much happiness, this much fulfillment, you want to share it with those you care about. I care about you—you are my brother, and I would like you to find the happiness I feel."

"Well, thank you. I hope we cross paths again sometime."

"And I as well." The captain leaned forward and added, "And I will pray for you. I will ask God to give you what you ask."

With that, the captain waved his hand and joined his crew in unloading and loading cargo.

18

Around noon, Simon exited the ship and set off on the ten-mile walk from the docks to his village. He'd easily be there by dinnertime.

As he crested the last hill on his approach, children playing nearby shouted with excitement, alerting everyone within hearing distance that someone was arriving. Soon he saw Mara walking out to greet him, just as she had every time he returned home from a long journey over the past three decades. For a moment his thoughts rushed back in time: she was nine months pregnant with Alexander and, oh, so beautiful! He looked at her now and thought her just as beautiful. Gray was slowly appearing in her dark hair. Lines near her eyes reminded him of all the smiles and happiness they had enjoyed. She walked with her arms extended out toward him.

His thoughts quickly turned to Alexander, who should have been with him at this moment and whom Mara was certainly expecting to see. He dreaded telling her what had happened between them.

"Welcome, welcome, my husband!" She enveloped his neck

and kissed his cheek. "You are home sooner than I thought you'd be. And where is Alexander?"

"He's fine. Nothing to worry about, but stories to share. He will be here in a few days. Let me get cleaned up, and perhaps we can eat, and then we will talk."

She knew him. She could hear in his voice all was not well, but she did not hear panic or fear, so she gave him his silence and they walked arm-in-arm to their home.

He had been right. He'd arrived home just before dinnertime, so his other children were all there, gathered near the table when he and Mara walked in. Rufus, five years younger than Alexander, was there with his pregnant wife, Batya. Simon's daughters, Miriam and Adinah, aged thirteen and eleven, stood and hugged him tightly. But only for a moment before ten-year-old Samuel, his youngest, pushed them aside and enthusiastically embraced his father.

Simon deposited his things and went to the well to wash. He tossed over and over in his mind how he would open the conversation. Should he involve the other children? Maybe just the older ones? Would Mara be upset or happy?

When he came back in, they were all at the table, ready for prayers. Simon took his seat at the head, grasped the hands of his children on either side of him, and closed his eyes. "Blessed are you, Lord our God, King of the earth, who creates fruit of the vine, fruit of the tree, and fruit of the earth. Oh, God, bless Alexander to return to us safely, and my thanks for keeping my family safe while I was gone. Amen."

"Amen," most of the family responded.

Simon looked up to see Mara staring at him. "Amen," she uttered softly, with a curious smile.

"So, stories to tell," Simon said quickly as he grabbed a piece of challah bread and started talking before anyone else could get a word in. He told them about the good prices he had received and how they had split up to take two different routes to Galilee, therefore making their profits better than any before in his long service.

"And Alexander—where is he?" Mara asked with just a hint of suspicion in her voice. Simon could tell she knew something wasn't quite right.

"He should be only a few days behind me. He stayed behind because . . ." Simon took another bite, trying to seem nonchalant. "He wanted to listen to the teachings of the man the entire country is talking about, the man they call Jesus."

The table was quiet. Simon kept eating, willing himself not to look up. While his heart had softened, he still was not sure how he felt about Alexander's decision. He didn't know what else to say. He worried that if he *did* say something it might sound angry. And so he decided he would not speak next, no matter what happened.

Finally, Mara looked at Rufus, gesturing to him to speak.

"Father, these teachings, as you call them, they are here as well. Many have come here who were present at his baptism by a man named John. They say something happened there. There was something they saw after the baptism, and then they heard a voice from heaven proclaiming him the Son of God."

Quiet again.

"Yes," Simon said. "That is what I heard too. And that's what has captured Alexander's imagination. He came through that area just after it happened. He walked many miles with some who witnessed it, and they told it exactly as you did. He was taken with their words, and he stayed. Jesus came to Tiberias, where we were, and he wanted to listen to him and to decide for himself." Simon stopped for a second. "Well, that is what *I* think he should do, but when he spoke to me, it sounded as though he had already decided."

"Decided what?" Mara asked.

"I think he has decided this is the Messiah, the one prophesied about. And he has based that decision on second- and thirdhand stories and on what he 'feels.'" The way Simon emphasized that last word revealed just how much doubt he had.

Mara did not miss a beat. "And, you, my husband. You heard him tell it. What are your feelings?"

Simon looked around the table. This was not a simple question.

"Something has happened while I was gone, hasn't it?"

Everyone looked at Rufus. "It has, Father. Apparently, right after John baptized him, Jesus went into the wilderness for several weeks, and no one heard from him. Then, when he came back, he began to teach. A new idea is now brought here by someone almost every day. He preaches of new commandments, of a different way of living. And every day we wait, hoping more will come up from the harbor with new experiences."

"I see. Well, let me reverse the question. What are your feelings?"

Rufus answered immediately. "Father, it's true. All of it. I know it."

"Because you feel it, correct?"

"Yes, because I feel it. It's not wanting it to be true, though I do. And it's not hoping it is true. It's an experience I have never had before. These feelings are so strong they are knowledge. And I feel I would offend God were I to say otherwise, because I think it is God sending these to me."

Simon just listened. When Rufus was done, Simon turned to Mara and raised a questioning eyebrow.

She stood from her seat and moved next to him. With her hands around his shoulders, she said, "Simon, I have always felt strongly that you and I are together on everything, and I think we have done well on that. But I cannot deny that, like Rufus, I have strong feelings. I feel as he does, and as completely as he does."

She looked around the table at their family. "Simon, we all do."

She then moved her hand to his cheek. "However, I can see you do not. Please don't let that come between us."

He patted her hand. "It will not. Nothing would."

She looked deep into his eyes. "But, my Simon, please give this a chance."

Perhaps it was his great love for Mara that caused him to do it. Or perhaps it was a small fleck of that feeling the others spoke of having. Whatever it was, he did something different than he'd ever done. He decided that this time he would not ignore what he didn't understand.

"I am not sure of anything," he said. "But I want you to tell me what you have heard, and why you are so sure."

Mara's eyes filled with tears as she leaned forward and threw her arms around him. The girls and Samuel got up and ran to him and did the same. Rufus stood behind him and grabbed his shoulders tightly. When they finished clasping each other, they went back to their seats, but each person was leaning a little closer to Simon

"Rufus," Mara said, "you speak."

For the next few hours, they shared each of the things they had heard, and what they felt, and why it mattered to them. Simon had to admit this felt better. He still did not know what *he* thought, but they were not at odds. They were excited, and he loved them so; he could listen because of that.

When they finished, it was late. The younger children retired to their beds, and Rufus and his wife returned to their home down the street. As Simon lay in bed with Mara, she held him tight but drifted off almost immediately. He looked at her. Her face was serene, almost smiling, and he would have guessed she was suppressing a laugh but for her deep breathing that let him know she was slumbering.

He stared at the ceiling. He did not know what to think. But he did know this—he loved his family and would try as hard as he could for them.

19

In the week leading up to Alexander's return home, Simon's family told him more and more about their feelings—and with increasing intensity. Once they knew Simon was open to listening, they couldn't resist. He had to smile at their passion. They each repeated the same things but used different ways to explain it all. He still wasn't sure he believed everything, but he no longer felt like he was defending a line in the sand.

The day before Alexander arrived, Simon was cleaning the animal stalls behind his home when Samuel came out and asked to help. He gave his youngest son a job suited to his age and then went about his own work. After a few minutes, Samuel stopped working and, in a hesitant manner, asked a question.

"Father, are you angry at us?"

Simon stopped immediately and squatted down to look at his son. "Samuel, why would you say that? I'm not angry at anything! I am so glad to be back with you. Have I done something to make you think I'm angry?"

Samuel's eyes filled with tears as he looked at him. "I was just worried."

"About what?"

"Everyone is so excited about Jesus. But you weren't here, and I did not know if you would be excited, and I was worried about our family . . ." His words trailed off and turned into sobs. He fell against his father, hugging him and burying his head in his shoulder.

"Samuel, Samuel," he said as he stroked his head. "Samuel, I'm excited too."

Samuel immediately picked his head up and looked at him.

"You are?" His eyes were red, but he was smiling. "You really are?"

Simon was perplexed for a minute. He did not want to lie to Samuel, but the boy's feelings were clearly fragile. He chose his words carefully. "Samuel, I am excited that our family is so excited. I am still learning, but can that be enough for now?"

The boy nodded.

Simon asked him again, "Why were you so worried?"

Samuel looked off to the side, his voice cracking. "My friend Asher and his brothers and sisters and mother have all listened to the stories from the people that come to our town too, and they all want to hear more, like we do. But their father does not. He gets more and more angry every time they talk about it, and a couple days ago, he said they couldn't listen to the stories anymore."

Samuel's eyes filled up with tears again, and his breathing became unsteady.

"Go on," Simon said gently.

"And now Asher is not supposed to play with me if I talk about it. And his father said if they kept believing, he would have to leave."

He took in a few sobbing breaths. "Father, I don't want our family to be angry at each other. I don't want us to be like that . . . I don't want you to leave us . . ."

Simon comforted him quietly for a few minutes. When it seemed Samuel had calmed down, Simon took him by the shoulders and held him at arm's length. "Samuel, that will never happen. Never! You are my family, and you are what I live for. You could never do anything that would make me leave. I give you my word that even if we all disagree about something, we will still be a family, and nothing will come between us."

He looked into Samuel's eyes. "Do you believe me, Samuel?"

Samuel smiled and nodded.

"Then that is that. So, now I need to ask you a question. How do you feel about all of this? Do you believe the stories?"

Samuel smiled, his eyes red. "They make me happy."

"Then that makes me happy," Simon said.

He tousled his son's hair and stood up. He watched proudly as Samuel went back to work. The boy was conscientious. He could also tell that a great burden had been lifted from him. He felt a sense of peace come over him as he committed to himself that he would do all he could to understand what was happening.

The very next day, his commitment was challenged.

20

While his family conversed enthusiastically and began making hurried plans, Simon sat stone-faced at the table.

Alexander had arrived that morning, just before the first meal, entering his parents' home with a giggling child wrapped around each leg, hand-in-hand with his wife. He greeted his father with a smile and his mother with a warm hug.

Simon smiled back at his oldest son, anxious to tell him how much had changed since they'd been together. He knew his son might be a little wary of him and cautious about upsetting him. As soon as they could be alone, he told himself, he would smooth things over.

During the meal, Alexander could not stop talking. He had followed Jesus from place to place for a week and was eager to share everything he'd learned. He said that wherever Jesus went, people crowded around him.

"He speaks of new commandments," Alexander said. "Of forgiveness and repentance and of watching out for our fellow man. Everywhere, he captivates people. Those of us following him compare our feelings, and it is the same. We are each filled with understanding—every one of us. I've never felt like this."

He looked at his wife, who smiled through her tears and said haltingly, "I understand. I feel it as well."

Alexander continued. "He calls it the Holy Ghost. It's not just a feeling, it's a spirit that can reside within us, and it testifies of truth to us. We could all feel it echoing inside."

Simon was captivated too. His mind raced with ideas. Then, suddenly, Alexander's voice faded into the background, and Simon recalled something with perfect clarity. He saw himself in the middle of the night, standing a short distance from a cave in Bethlehem. He recalled the feeling that had come over him that night as he'd watched the shepherds gazing in a awe at a newborn baby. It was a feeling of peace and reassurance. *After all these years,* he thought to himself, *that memory is so clear.*

"And," Alexander said, "that is not all. He performs miracles."

Simon's attention turned back to his son's voice.

"Not one but many! There was a wedding in Cana just before I found him, in which to honor the bride and bridegroom he changed water into wine."

The family held their breath.

"At first I couldn't believe it myself, but there were several with us who had attended the wedding, and they swore it was true."

Simon could feel something—trouble, suspicion maybe?— begin to rise within him. *Water into wine,* he thought cynically. *It's starting to sound like the stories that were exaggerated by travelers around fires on the road.*

"He healed the son of an official at Capernaum," Alex shared excitedly.

"You saw this one?" Simon asked.

The joy evident in Alexander's face darkened a little. "I did not, Father. But these people with me, who I trust, they did."

Simon forced a smile and said nothing. He felt some tension return between him and Alexander. Fortunately, nobody else seemed to notice it.

Simon willed himself to let it go, and it eased some.

But not for long.

"The most important news is this," Alexander said carefully. "And, Devorah, I have not spoken with you yet, so I am sorry for bringing this up with the whole family present, but, well . . ."

"Go ahead," she said. "There's nothing you can say that they cannot hear. And I believe I know what you will say."

Alexander smiled at her, then turned to his family. "On the next to last day I was there, Jesus was teaching by the seashore, by the Sea of Galilee. He told us the time had come for the kingdom of God on earth to be established. We need to repent, he said, and believe what he teaches us and follow him . . ."

Simon cut in, trying to mask the hint of challenge in his voice. "Most of these things he teaches—how we should act and treat others—they make sense to me. And telling us to repent is sound advice. But can't we be good people—aren't we still good people— without believing *everything* he is saying? Must we embrace it all?"

Alexander seemed to notice his father's effort to remain open and unchallenging. "Father, that is a good question. I think it all comes down to faith. Jesus says this is the most basic doctrine. If we have faith in God and faith that Jesus is his son, we will follow him—follow all of his ways. And this faith will give us power . . .

and joy. Joy that is greater than anything you can imagine! Power to do his work and change our lives—and others' lives."

Simon persisted. "But, why? Why does the power come from that? If God loves us, and I believe he does, why don't we have that power?"

Alexander responded lovingly. "Father, I don't know what it all means yet, and likely never will. But he's taught this, and I believe it. If complete faith is what is asked of me, that is what I will give."

"And," Alexander said, looking back at Devorah, "that is what I wanted to tell you. While there, he went to these fishermen and spoke with them. I couldn't hear his words, but they later told us that he had asked them to leave their nets and follow him. Not for a while but forever! And do you know what these men did? They looked at him and stopped what they were doing! There were four of them, three young, one older. The older one reached down and put his hands in the water, then stood, wiped them on his cloak, and started walking behind Jesus down the beach. Just like that!"

He continued. "I hear his voice in my heart, asking me to do whatever I can to serve him. So, Devorah, I believe we need to go to Galilee, all of us. There is so much to do, and I want to be a part of it."

The family gasped, and Simon's face turned to stone. Everyone looked at Devorah, who was quiet.

Her eyes welled up. "Alexander, I have been praying these last few weeks. When people came through the town—believers and followers—and told us of what was happening, I felt the call to be there, to help. I have been praying that you would be touched as well. I have had something, someone, tell me clearly that you would be affected this way on your trip with Simon. I was told that I must be sure, and if I was, that I must be ready. When your father told us of the baptism of Jesus and that you were staying, I knew my prayers were answered, and I have been preparing. When you are ready, I am. We all are."

Everyone began talking excitedly at once. Simon remained frozen in place. Why was this happening? Why would his son leave them, leave his birthplace to . . . ? And what was this emotion welling up in him? Sadness? Anger? Hurt? Something else entirely? He did not know. He didn't understand what was happening; it was just too much. And though he sincerely did not want to draw attention to himself, he felt an urgent need to be alone to sift through his thoughts. Quietly, he stood and walked out the rear door of their house and into their stable area.

When he turned to the south, he could see the sea in the distance and the ships, ever so small, moving in and out of port as the sun glistened off the waters. Inside his home, his world had just turned inside out. But out here, everything was just as it had always been—moving forward at its own pace, ignorant of Alexander's decision, his family's reaction, and everything it meant to Simon's life. This feeling comforted him but also chastised him, reminding him that the world did not revolve around him.

He stood for a while—he did not know for how long—blocking everything from his mind but the view down the hillside.

At one point he heard someone come up behind him. Thirty-plus years of caring about his wife had given him an uncanny ability to recognize the sound of her walk, the cadence of her movements, and the rustling swish of her robes as they brushed the ground. He felt a sense of familiarity and relief as her gentle hand found its way around his waist and she rested her head on his shoulder. They stood together in comfortable silence for another while.

He spoke first. "I suppose you feel this is a good idea?"

She rubbed his back for a moment, then answered. "If feel sure that Alexander feels sure. I feel Devorah has heard rightly the answer to her prayers. If these are true, then I feel it is a good idea for them."

"And for us?" he said as he turned to look at her.

"Unless I am missing something, I do not think you have heard the same call." She stopped there and let it settle.

"No, I've not." He laughed under his breath, but not with humor. "Not even close."

"Then our place is here, together."

He was not worthy of this woman! He'd felt this way since the day they'd married, and the thought came rushing back to him again, all at once. He turned toward her and took her by the shoulders. "But what would you do if it were not for me?"

She did as she always did when her husband needed comfort. She put both of her hands on his cheeks. It was, he thought, the greatest expression of love she showed him. "If it were not for you, I would be sad. I would not have these beautiful children. I would not have my comfortable home. I would not have this man as my husband, a man who is strong in his values and dedicated to us."

"That is not what I meant," he protested.

"I know exactly what you meant," she responded. "And this is what I mean. If you have not heard that call, then my place, all our places, are here, together."

Simon was surprised at what happened next. He broke down in tears, his arms tight around Mara. He cried—hard. Not a word passed between them, but he knew she understood it all.

She just held him silently until it was time for evening prayers.

21

The following morning, Simon was out tending to the animals as the sun came up. He heard a noise and turned to see Alexander. He had known this moment would come and thought quickly through how he wanted to appear. He turned, stood tall, and gave his son a smile.

"So, my son, how soon will you be leaving?" Despite the deliberate effort, he did not quite sound cheery, but he did sound supportive.

"Tomorrow morning, Father. We will, of course, go by ship. Passover is coming, and the captains are taking advantage of it. There will be many ships."

"Yes," Simon said, "and they will make you pay for the privilege."

"I know." Alexander laughed. "We can manage. It's time, and it will get us there."

There was silence for a moment, and then Alexander said, "Father, obviously you realize that I will no longer be a merchant with you . . ."

"Oh!" Simon exclaimed. "That reminds me. I have your

earnings from our last journey. You will need those." He started to turn into the house, but Alexander grabbed his arm and stopped him.

"Father, that is not why I said that. I have my earnings. Those are yours. Keep them . . ."

"No, we have a business, good and fair. These are yours and I want to give them to you." Simon walked into the house and returned with a leather pouch he handed to his son.

Alexander weighed the bag in his hand. "You know this is not fair. This is too much."

"It seems to me," Simon said with false sternness, while he returned to brushing down the cow, "that though we were partners, I was in charge, was I not? So don't challenge me. That is your share."

His son just smiled and nodded. "Thank you." He looked at his father for a moment, and then emotion welled up. "I want you to know I have loved working with you. I . . ."

Simon slowly spread his arms toward his son. They embraced, and both men sobbed. Simon put one hand on the back of his son's head and held him firm, which just made them both shake harder. There was no sound. Simon could think of only one thing: he wanted his son to know that he loved him. That was more important than anything he was struggling with.

Inside their home, Mara stood quietly, peeking around the edge of the door. She stifled her own tears and quietly offered a thank-you to God for answering her prayer.

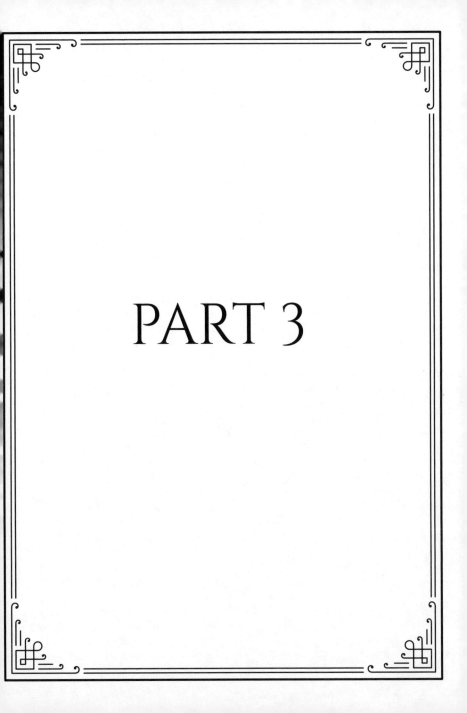

PART 3

22

And so Simon found a new balance in his life. Rufus had decided long before this time that his destiny was not to follow his father's vocation. He had found a trade in town as a carpenter. Simon was proud of him. The years on the road with Alexander had been a special time, and he missed that, but he had never wanted his children to choose that way of life simply because he had. It was a hard lifestyle from a family standpoint. Mara had long ago found a way to make it work, but it was not for everyone. Besides, Rufus having a carpentry shop in town meant he was nearby to look after Simon's family when he was traveling.

The number of followers of Jesus in their community was growing slowly but steadily. It surprised Simon a little that this could happen so far from Galilee. But the influence of this man seemed to have no boundaries. Rufus, like Alexander, was a complete believer and had become somewhat of a . . . *what?* Simon was not sure what to call him. Rufus had a knowledge of the scriptures that Simon could take no credit for. When he spoke, people listened to him. He was not bold, but was quiet and sure of himself and patient, and his carpentry shop was often crowded with people just wanting to ask questions while he worked. He never was too busy to stop and spend time with someone who sincerely wanted to understand.

He told Simon his work teaching Jesus's principles was that of an apprentice—his knowledge was nowhere close to that of the Master, but he was learning and trying. He called it being a disciple.

Over the next several months, Simon made many trips but tried to keep them shorter. He found he could go out for a only few weeks at a time. He went more often; it seemed to work out, and he was able to provide. There was so much happening, and he wanted to stay close to what Mara was learning. One evening, he was helping Mara clean up the evening meal when he casually mentioned his next journey.

"You know how popular silphium is in Galilee?"

"Yes, of course," she said. "It has meant so much to your business I think we should have named one of the children Silphium to honor it." Mara laughed, and it made Simon laugh.

"Well, as you know, the supply is good right now. And the farther I get from here, the better prices I can get. So I will be leaving in a few days." She stopped but did not look up.

"And I thought I would go to Galilee. They seem to have a great fondness for it there. And . . ."

She turned and looked anxiously at him.

"And . . . I thought as long as I was there, I might wander up to Capernaum . . ."

"Do you think you could find him?" she interrupted.

"Who?" said Simon, feigning confusion.

She turned from where she was putting away food. "The girls

and I will start preparing some things for them right now." She walked away, calling her daughters.

He called after her. "There is no guarantee, you know."

"You'll find him," she said simply. I know it."

Simon looked at her quizzically. "Are you referring to Alexander, or . . ." He let the words hang.

Mara went back to her work with a satisfied grin, saying nothing.

23

Simon had filled his bags with as much of the rare spice as he could. In his hip pouch, he carried small gifts and letters from his family to Alexander and his wife and children. When his ship docked in Tyre a few days later, he wondered if it had been perhaps foolish to give Mara so much hope. These lands were not small. *Would it even be possible to find his son?* And then he remembered what Alexander had said some months earlier, before he and his young family departed: "Ask after Jesus. Wherever he is, you will find me."

Simon purchased his animals and made a decision. The profitable thing to do would have been to sell his way through each town on the way to Capernaum. Such a journey would take ten days at least, maybe two weeks. But he felt a sense of urgency, not anxiety or worry, just the need to act quickly. He did as Alexander suggested, and while still in Tyre, he inquired about the Messiah and where he might be found. Each person he asked pointed toward Capernaum.

I knew it would be Capernaum, Simon mused with awe.

He started out right away, pushing his beasts as hard as was possible. After only two nights on the road, he arrived.

The city was busy. He could tell right away that many walking the streets were visitors. Clothing styles marked a foreigner, and he recognized many robes, tunics, and footwear from other regions of the Empire; there were even some he had never seen before. He went about securing a room for the night, settled his animals, and then set out with his hip bag to explore the city.

Capernaum was a maze of streets—walkways converging and diverging again and again. Simon had no idea where to go. After a few minutes, he did not even know where he was. As he walked, he could hear Mara's voice in his mind, telling him she *knew* he would find Alexander. He noticed a section in a nearby wall where the stone curved inward slightly, creating a small spot to step off the road. There, he leaned against the wall and self-consciously lowered his head slightly. He hoped any who looked his way would think he was contemplating the dirt at his feet. Ever so slightly, with barely a breath, he prayed.

"Adonay . . ."

Simon immediately stopped. It struck him that he had not uttered God's name in that way in decades. At the table in his home and on the Sabbath when he led his family in prayer, he used the name, but it was always formal, if not cold. When he was a child, he had loved to hear his father pray. When his father spoke the name *Adonay*, it always seemed like he was referring to a beloved friend. It was gentle, respectful, and almost familiar. Today Simon realized his relationship with the Almighty was changing. He too had just addressed God as a friend. He continued.

"Adonay, you know Mara feels so strongly that I will find Alexander. And you know that I felt I should come to Capernaum."

He paused once more and quietly laughed at himself. *Felt!* He recalled the near disdain that had often broiled inside him when someone else claimed to base their belief in Jesus on what they had felt. But here he was, praying on the road after traveling hundreds and hundreds of miles—all because of a feeling.

"Adonay, I have felt this, and I could be wrong. But I know you love Mara, and it would mean a great deal if I could find our son."

There were many passersby on the road in front of him, their words blending together into a constant hum. Suddenly, two voices stood out. Simon could hear them clearly, right in front of him, as if they were actually speaking to him.

"Where?" one voice questioned.

"The plaza. Alexander said he would be teaching there this afternoon," the other replied.

Simon immediately opened his eyes to identify the speakers. He saw two men walking away, still talking, and recognized one of the voices as the first he'd just heard. He hurried behind them, keeping close, so as to not lose sight of them.

They led him past three walkways and then out to a junction of alleyways that formed a large, open courtyard. Simon looked around to see buildings and merchants lining the perimeter on all sides of the open space. There were many spice tables here, and he might have done well, but stopping to sell his goods did not even occur to him.

He was too busy searching, hoping he might find Alexander here. It was then he heard a familiar voice. After another moment of searching, he located it. There was Alexander! *His son!* Sitting on a wall near the well at the center of the crowd. Simon stepped into the shadows where he could hear but would be hidden from Alexander's direct line of sight.

The first questions from the crowd were challenging, even somewhat antagonistic, Simon thought. But Alexander seemed to remain perfectly calm.

"But it is the Sabbath!" someone shouted out. "Regardless of what you say, we have been commanded to keep the Sabbath holy."

"You are correct," Alexander said. "And you—and all of us!—are blessed when we keep this commandment. But the Master asks us to remember that God made the Sabbath, and he made it for us. He has taught, 'Man was not created for the Sabbath.'

"I listened recently as Jesus asked this: 'Who among you if you have a sheep, and it falls into a pit on the Sabbath would not lift it out?'

"If you are sick, and the Master can bless and heal you on the Sabbath, are you not better than a sheep?"

Someone called out, "I am!"

Alexander laughed. "You are, my friend! And you all are!" He looked out, waving his hand across the crowd and making eye contact with as many as he could. In doing so, he found his father's face among the many others watching him.

"Come hear him tomorrow," Alexander challenged the crowd. His words came out just a little more quickly than before. "Listen to what he says and see if it does not prick your heart."

Alexander stood up before any in the crowd could further question him and made his way to Simon.

"Father!" he exclaimed, his arms wrapping Simon in a warm embrace. "I didn't expect you here. This is a great surprise."

"You know . . . business." Simon smiled. "How is your family?"

Alexander beckoned his father to walk with him. "We are all well. All well. They will be excited to see you."

"How are you getting along? Surely they are not paying you to teach?"

"Oh no," Alexander said, still smiling. "Of course not. I do this out of love. That is my pay. But because of all the good things you taught me, I am able to bargain well with the traveling merchants, and I sell in the markets. Sometimes fruits and vegetables, sometimes spices."

Alexander's eyes sparkled as he continued. "It almost feels like I am deceiving them now that I am on the other side of the table and know all their tricks and techniques. I am making enough, and it is easy for the family to pack up and move when Jesus moves. We have been down to Jerusalem and back since we got here—" He paused.

"Father, how did you know to look for us here? Just two weeks ago we were in the Holy City."

"I just felt I would find you here," Simon said, realizing immediately that he had used *that* word again. He saw Alexander break into a knowing smile.

"You *felt* it?" Alexander asked, his eyebrows raised.

"I'm still your father. You need to show respect," Simon said with a wink.

"Come," Alexander said, "let me take you to our home."

They walked through the crowded streets, talking about whatever came to mind—the city, the changing times in Israel and Judah, the Romans.

When they came to Alexander's home, Simon saw that it was nothing more than a room in someone else's house. It was adequate, true; there was a place to cook, room to sleep, and it was clean and safe. But . . .

His thoughts were interrupted by Devorah and his grandchildren, who exploded with excitement when he came in. The little ones crawled all over him. He couldn't get enough of it, and he laughed heartily.

"How long will you be here?" Devorah asked.

"Oh, just a day or so. I have gifts for you from Mara and the children." He took off his hip bag and passed them out.

That evening, Devorah made a meal out of what seemed to be nothing. Simon thought of offering to buy some food for them, but they made no complaint, or any excuse, and he did not want to offend them. After the meal, the children wandered out to play, and Alexander, Devorah, and Simon sat and enjoyed the peace of the evening. They asked about each family member one by one, with Simon telling them everything he could. They were particularly interested in what Rufus was doing and wanted to hear details of what he was teaching and how he answered difficult questions.

"So," Simon asked. "How goes your work here?"

"You mean as a merchant?"

"No, you told me about that. I mean your . . . other work. The work that brought you here."

Alexander looked surprised. "Father, you're interested?"

"I am. You're my son, and this matters to you, so it matters to me."

"Well," Alexander replied, obviously pleased. "You ask on a special day."

"A holiday of some sort?"

Alexander became very serious. "Father, of all the times I have listened, learned, and studied thus far, today was the most powerful. Everything I believe, we believe, everything we have done, made sense today."

"Made sense?" Simon asked. "I thought it already made sense. Isn't that why you came?"

Alexander shook his head. "Of course, you are right, it has made sense. But today it made more sense. That's how this has gone. You hear a truth and it leaves you speechless. You feel it may be the most important thing you have ever learned. Then you learn another, and you realize the first idea was merely a foundation upon which the next should be placed. And so it goes."

"So what happened today?"

"This morning, Jesus was preparing to teach by the sea, but the crowds were incredible. People seemed to come from everywhere. There were rich and poor, old and young, and people from countries unfamiliar to me. He realized there was no way to address them all, and he led us along the road to a low mountain near here. He sat on a rock, and the people sat all over the mountainside to listen. And then he began to teach."

Alexander had to take a deep breath.

"There is so much I don't even know where to begin. I cannot even remember it all. Let me begin with this: he said that the meek will be blessed and inherit the earth."

Simon looked confused. "The meek? Why would they inherit the earth?"

Alexander answered. "I believe he means the humble. That their humility will be rewarded in time, sometime."

"That is hard to understand," Simon replied.

"I know. But let me share several parts of it. If you hear it all together, it might help."

Alexander closed his eyes to try to say it slowly and perfectly. "Blessed are the poor in spirit, for theirs is the kingdom of heaven. Blessed are they that mourn, for they shall be comforted. Blessed are the meek, for they shall inherit the earth. Blessed are they which do hunger and thirst after righteousness, for they shall be filled. Blessed are the merciful, for they shall obtain mercy. Blessed are the pure in heart, for they shall see God. Blessed are the peacemakers, for they shall be called the children of God. Blessed are they which are persecuted for righteousness' sake, for theirs is the kingdom of heaven. Blessed are ye, when men shall revile you, and persecute you, and shall say all manner of evil against you falsely, for my sake. Rejoice, and be exceeding glad, for great is your reward in heaven, for so persecuted they the prophets which were before."

The room was quiet. Simon looked down for a long time, something welling up inside him.

Alexander and Devorah waited patiently.

"This is what you meant, isn't it?" Simon finally asked. "This feeling I have now, *this* is what you felt? This is how you knew it to be true when you first learned about Jesus and his baptism by John?"

Alexander nodded, smiling through the tears that flowed freely down his cheeks.

Simon spoke again. "This feeling . . . it is what you call the Holy Ghost?"

"Yes. The Holy Ghost! He is sent to us in the name of the Messiah to testify whenever there is truth. He has promised us that the Spirit will teach us all things," Alexander responded.

Simon recalled the conversation he'd had with the captain months before and said quietly, "When we are taught that if we *ask*, he will answer . . . is it through this spirit that he will answer?"

Alexander exclaimed, "Yes, yes! Father, Jesus does not ask us to accept his teachings without proof. There is proof! It is this spirit that is the proof. But it is not proof in the worldly sense."

At that moment, Simon remembered something. *The cave. Bethlehem. The shepherds.* He was suddenly there, but not as he'd been before. More than thirty years ago, when he had stood outside that cave in Bethlehem, he stood on the periphery, watching from a distance. But tonight he was in the middle of it. He grabbed his son's and Devorah's hands fiercely, as if to hold on to the feelings in the room. Three decades of listening, thinking, and questioning converged. Suddenly, somehow, he knew he was ready for something more.

Silently, in his heart, he asked.

Within his heart, it was given him.

24

In the morning, Simon packed up his animals and returned to Alexander's home.

As soon as Alexander saw him, he looked surprised. "I thought you were staying a day or two?"

Simon finished tying up his animals in the courtyard. "I did. And I decided to stay a day, not two."

Alexander looked uncomfortable. "Are you bothered by our conversation last night?"

"No, no, no," Simon said as he put his arm around his son's shoulders. "No, not at all. I just would like to think about it for a while. I can do that better as I move on again."

Alexander seemed disappointed. "Of course, that is your decision. However, I have an idea. How would you like to go hear Jesus speak today?"

"I thought of that," Simon said. "But I am not ready. Last night was beyond comprehension for me. I need to ponder it more."

Alexander responded quickly. "Father, we don't need to speak with him or even stand close to him. But given all you have felt, don't you want to actually hear him for yourself?"

Simon sighed. "I do, my son, I really do. It is hard to explain, but it's too soon."

As he said it, he knew it sounded disingenuous. But he couldn't say out loud that he was afraid. It was his fear that was too hard to explain.

Alexander looked to his wife somewhat pleadingly, hoping she could say something to change his mind.

She turned to face Simon but spoke to Alexander. "This is a personal journey for all of us, Alexander. I think your father will know what to do and when to do it."

Then, directing her comments to Simon, she added, "Father, I have never been happier than having you with us as these things have come close to your heart. Please, come be with us as often as you can, for as long as you like. Our home is your home"—she smiled before going on—"wherever that happens to be at the moment."

Simon nodded and thanked his daughter-in-law by clasping her hand between his.

He then addressed Alexander. "Son, please try to understand. Everything you have given me has meant so much, and I will pursue it. But at this point, I would like to get on my way, finish my trip, and return home to your mother."

"Well, to be honest, I don't understand," Alexander said, trying not to sound frustrated. "But you know I support whatever you need to do."

"All right then," Simon said with a quick change of tone. "Where are my grandchildren?"

He found them out back, and they each hugged him long and hard, begging him to stay.

"I will be back. Don't worry."

He gathered his few things and went to his animals in the yard. Alexander and Devorah followed him out. He thanked them both, promising one more time to return soon. And then he backed slowly out of their yard, keeping his eyes on them until the last second. It was not lost on him that not far from here, not that long ago, he had left Alexander, but with his back turned—both literally and figuratively. On that day he was silently and intentionally sending a message of disapproval. On this day, he desired to overcome that memory, to replace it. When he reached the road, he waved his arm high over his head and yelled, "Shalom!" with as big a smile as he felt.

The contrast did not appear to be lost on Alexander either, who said the same thing he had at that last parting. Last time it felt to Simon like a plea, but this time it seemed an affirmation. "Shalom, Father! And God be with you until we meet again."

Simon turned, satisfied and peaceful, and began his journey.

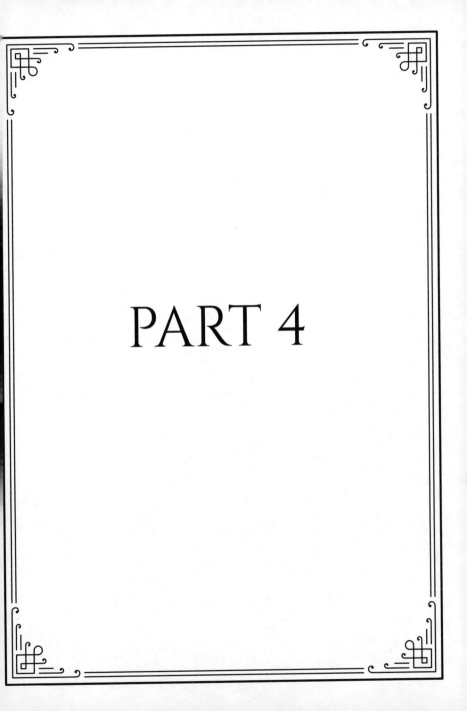

PART 4

25

As word spread of Jesus's teachings, Simon now actively sought out news. In the villages, as he sold his spices, he asked what others had heard. Sometimes he found people like him, who were also seeking; and their discussions would go on for hours. Other times he met individuals who disdained such talk and despised "that man"; those conversations would end abruptly. Though he was not proficient at it yet, he tried to respond to the latter with a smile and a kind word.

Sometimes he met those who seemed unsure and confused or who wore suspicion on their faces as a facade for their lack of confidence. It was these he enjoyed finding most. He worked hard to comfort them by explaining that he was just a step or two ahead of them on the path—that he had been right where they were. He affirmed their need to question and that they were still good people if they had not yet decided what to believe. He then would gently ask if they wanted to know what had changed him. "If only as something to think about," he'd add. Usually, cautiously, they would say yes, looking around them as if to be sure no one else could hear. He would offer to sit with them and, again and again, he would explain that this was only his story, that each man and woman must travel this road in their own way. But if he could help, he was happy to do so. He also assured them there was still much he did not know. He was never hesitant to admit he didn't know the answer to a question. He promised on these occasions that the next time he was with a true follower, he would ask for answers—and that they should too.

Humility had not been unknown to Simon in the past, but now it surfaced in a new and more vibrant way. His humility encouraged him, it brought him joy, and it made him an enthusiastic student. He loved camping with others along the side of the road and talking with them late into the evening. *Something happens around a fire in the night,* he often thought. *People seem so much more willing to share their feelings.* As he sat with fellow travelers, acquaintances for no more than an evening, there would frequently be both doubters and believers with him. He learned much as he listened to other believers explain Jesus's teachings to those who were more skeptical.

He started to restrict his travel to the areas of Judea, Samaria, and Galilee—where Jesus was also spending his time. When traveling these roads, Simon could get news that was only days'—sometimes hours—old, rather than the weeks' old news he got in regions closer to his home. He stayed abreast of exactly where the Messiah was whenever possible, because he knew there he would also find Alexander.

Sometimes at the roadside encampments, his newfound friends would ask if he had seen Jesus. When he said no, they would excitedly tell him where he might find him. He always thanked them but never sought him out.

When Simon finally returned home, he brought the latest news of Jesus: his healings of the sick, his profound parables, his miraculous feeding of the multitudes with only a few loaves and fishes, his raising of the dead, and the men he called apostles, who came from very different backgrounds but were united in their complete and total devotion to his teachings.

At home, Simon was likewise able to catch up on the happenings there. Rufus had contributed to building a small community of followers. In fact, many referred to his carpentry shop as a synagogue, much to the dismay of the orthodox in town. Rufus assured all who were interested that it was nothing but a tradesman's workplace, and then continued his teaching and listening and comforting of those who came while he worked the wood.

The weeks turned into months. Before Simon realized it, almost three years had passed since Alexander had encountered the witnesses of Jesus's baptism and learned about the gospel.

Simon returned to the road, never tiring of his encounters there. He began to feel like he had heard most of the questions people had and that he was prepared with answers. Though his life had changed, he found comfort in the predictability of his new existence. So it was surprising to him when one evening, something gave him pause.

He was west of Jerusalem, near Lydda. Evening had come, and he was settled around a fire with three other men, none of whom knew each other. When Simon was near the Holy City, or anywhere in Galilee, he seemed to hear nothing but stories of Jesus, and this night was no different. One of the men asked Simon question after question, seemingly focused on learning everything that

Simon believed. Simon was enjoying sharing his experiences when the man interrupted him.

"So you must be a disciple?"

Simon stopped. He knew of disciples. He spoke of disciples. But he had never considered himself one. He answered, but tentatively.

"I am a follower, if that's what you mean."

The man sensed Simon's brief hesitation and quickly asked another.

"No, that's not what I mean. I mean, are you a disciple?"

Simon looked at him, unsure what to say next.

The other man grabbed a stick and poked at the embers of the fire. "You are not, then." It was more a statement than a question.

At first Simon was not comfortable being called a disciple. Now he wondered if he should be offended that this man did not think him one.

Simon's confusion showed as he tried to explain himself. "I believe what Jesus teaches. I try to keep the commandments as I know them, and though I have much to learn, I do my best."

The other man just kept looking down into the fire, shaking his head. "No, you are not a disciple."

Simon replied sharply, "Why do you say that?"

The man looked at him. "It offends you that I know you are not a disciple?"

There was no apology in the man's tone. Nor did he seem to be prodding Simon. He seemed more factual than anything else.

Simon decided he was making it worse by talking, and instead poked at the embers as well. The tension was palpable, and the other two men, silent so far, looked at each other before standing to go tend to their animals.

The man went on. "These men, these disciples, I think they are excessive. Some of his apostles are supposedly fishermen, or at least they were. Jesus told them to leave their nets, and they did, without hesitation. I don't know what Jesus does for food or to afford a place to sleep, but apparently he doesn't care if anyone else has to find a way to provide."

The man looked up again. "What he teaches is fine. But he does not seem to acknowledge there are lives to be lived, responsibilities, needs."

Simon paused, not knowing what to think.

"So what makes you say I am not a disciple?" Simon asked.

The man looked up, almost surprised. He waved his hands at the animals. "You are a merchant, like I am. You are working. You haven't walked away from your vocation to follow him."

Simon replied, still unsure what to think, "And you feel everyone must do that to be a disciple?"

"Seems so," the man said. "These people who follow him in droves, I don't know how they can work if they are there, every day, listening to him."

Simon stared into the fire, not seeing anything.

"And this meal," the man said.

Simon looked up. "What do you mean?"

"You cooked your food awhile ago, and then you ate it."

"Disciples don't eat food?" Simon asked sarcastically.

"Of course they do, but they bless it first. I didn't see you do that."

Simon replied, his voice weak, "I do when at home."

Now the man looked at him and then laughed out loud. "That, my fellow merchant is not discipleship—that is wisdom! I do too, and, as you know, that keeps a wife happy. Out here it doesn't matter."

Simon did not answer. The man kept talking, but Simon didn't hear a word he said.

26

For the rest of the trip, Simon rarely conversed with others in the evening. When possible, he found rooms where he could be alone. When he could not secure a room, he either sat by himself at the roadside camp or joined a big group where he could remain silent and unnoticed.

When he returned home, he met Mara at the outskirts of town. It had become their tradition, so much so that he would delay coming into the village just to enjoy the anticipation of waiting for her. She came to him with open arms and hugged him. Then, as if she could sense something, she took him by the shoulders and held him at arm's length.

"What is it, Simon?"

"What is what?"

He feigned ignorance, but he was terrible at concealing anything from Mara.

"Something is troubling you. Did something go wrong on your trip?"

"It was good enough."

He took her arm and began walking back. She clasped his hand but gave him his silence.

◆ ◆ ◆

The following evening, Rufus and his family joined Simon, Mara, and their other children for dinner. Rufus updated him on all that had been happening in town, but when he asked Simon about his own travels, the father said little.

"I did not see Alexander and Devorah this time, and it was mostly all trading, so not much to share."

Rufus found that odd and looked at his father questioningly until he saw Mara signal with a slight shake of her head to go no further.

After the sun set, they retired to the roof and the cool evening air. Eventually, conversation was replaced with quiet. Some time later, Rufus asked, "Father and Mother, may I ask you something?"

Mara looked at him inquisitively. Simon just continued staring into the sky.

"What would you give up to follow him?"

He let the question hang in the silence.

Simon froze. At first he wondered if Mara had said something to Rufus, but then he remembered that he had told her nothing of it himself.

"It would be easy to say 'everything,'" Mara said, stirring Simon from his thoughts.

"I believe I feel that," she continued, "but I have not been asked to do so, so I am not sure. I hope I would."

Simon said nothing.

"Father?" Rufus asked after a while.

"Why do you ask me that?"

Rufus could likely tell he had touched on a delicate subject for Simon. Again, Mara signaled him; but this time he ignored her warning.

"First of all, I did not ask just you. I asked you both. Second, I have been thinking about it. A man came through town a week ago, and he found his way to my shop. He shared a story I had not heard before."

"A parable?" Simon asked.

"No, not this time. He said he was in a crowd and witnessed this when it happened. A man had come to Jesus asking for guidance. He appeared to be a man of means, perhaps even a government official of some kind. He wore fine clothing and had some men with him who seemed to be his servants. Despite his wealth, the man seemed quite humble and sincere. He referred to Jesus as 'Master' and then began asking him what he needed to do to gain eternal life."

Rufus paused.

"Go on," Simon said quietly.

"Well, Jesus told him to keep the commandments. This man asked him which ones, and Jesus began quoting the commandments given to Moses. The man then replied that he had done those things and asked what he still lacked."

Again Rufus stopped.

Simon turned his head toward his son. Well?" he asked expectantly.

"He told the man to sell all that he had, to give his proceeds to the poor, and then to follow him."

Simon now sat up. "And did he?"

"No," Rufus said. "This surprised the man who spoke to us. He said this ruler had seemed so dedicated. But when Jesus told him those things, he only looked forlorn and, without a word, walked away."

"Do you think that's fair?" Simon asked, sounding troubled.

"I definitely agree that it seems hard," Rufus responded. "But the man *was* asking what he could do to gain eternal life. Seems to me that the value of the desired gift is significantly greater than what Jesus was asking him to give up, don't you think?"

"Of course, but still . . ." Simon's words drifted off.

"But still what?" Rufus would not let it drop.

Simon tried to organize his thoughts.

"It's like your mother said, it's easy to *say* you would give up everything. I think it would be much harder to *do*."

He paused, then continued. "Rufus, you ask these questions and say these things so easily. Are you sure you are really meaning what you say? You would give up your carpentry shop without a second thought if Jesus came and asked you to follow him?"

"He has, Father."

"What? When was he here?"

Rufus shook his head. "No, he wasn't here. But he has asked every one of us that question through so many of his parables and admonitions. He has asked us to leave our nets, leave our homes, take up our crosses, and follow him. When I heard it asked the first time and understood that we all must to be able to answer the question if we are to become true followers, I started thinking about it. I had to take time and really consider if I meant it. I had to picture it, to test myself, to talk to Batya, and then to pray and ask God to help me understand my feelings."

"And I suppose you must have become convinced?"

"I have. I wish I could explain this better, but after I thought about it all I could, I asked God to help me know if I meant it, if I could really do it."

"And what did he say?" Simon asked.

"He didn't *say* anything, but he gave me an answer. I offered the prayer I just described to you one evening after a few months of questioning myself and pondering the idea. When I went to sleep, I was not sure, but I knew that God would let me know where I stood with him. And if I was lacking, I would keep working on it. However, when I awoke, there was this certainty in my heart. Father, I knew! I knew beyond any doubt that I could do it."

"So, then," Simon asked, "why are you still here?" He was almost scowling.

"I thought about leaving, as Alexander has done, about just giving my shop to someone and taking the family and going to find Jesus. But something important occurred to me. I don't believe he is asking every person to physically leave their professions and walk with him. He is the Son of God, but still he grows older. He was a baby once, then a child, and now a man. I assume he will grow older and older and die someday. If he does, how will we follow him them? How will those who come after us follow him? I don't think these commandments are only for when he is here with us."

Simon's interest was growing.

"So what did you decide?" he asked.

The two men were now sitting cross-legged and facing each

other. Mara sat just behind Simon, and Batya just behind Rufus. The two women exchanged small smiles. Mara then looked at Rufus and gently nodded, encouraging him to continue.

"I think it is this, Father. For some, really a few, he wants them to literally follow him, walk with him, assist him in his work. But for most of us, he means for us to follow him by living the way he is asking us to, by keeping the commandments he gives us, by treating others the way he would. Really, by emulating as well as we are able all he does. This is why I stayed. This is why I keep my shop. Every day, people come to sit and discuss the Master's teachings. I help them understand when I can, and by doing that, I am sharing his words, and I am following him."

Batya interrupted him. "Father, you should know that Rufus is considered a great teacher, and people hear about him and come from long distances to ask him questions. He has become a leader in this movement."

"Rufus, if I wanted to do what you have done, to really know if I would follow him, would I just do as you have?"

"Yes," Rufus answered, without sitting up. "That is the way he taught us. Do all you can and then prayerfully ask God. He will tell you."

Simon sat quietly thinking about his answer, and Rufus asked, "Is there more on your mind, Father?"

Simon responded, "You said something about 'taking up a cross.' Are you referring to a crucifixion?"

Rufus now sat up on one elbow. "Father, I have prayed about this as well. I don't think he literally means for us to be crucified, but I think it is a symbol to represent death. The question is would we be willing to die for him."

"A crucifixion is a Roman atrocity. It's torture. It is a terrible way to die," Simon said with great seriousness.

"Yes, I know. But I suppose if you can answer yes to dying that way, you're sincere about dying if he asks you to for his sake."

Simon lay back down. "If that is Jesus's intent, to make the question as difficult as possible, then he was successful. I have seen a crucifixion. Only once, but I wish I had not. I cannot get the memory out of my mind."

With that, the conversation ended for the evening. The four adults looked at the stars for a while more, and then Rufus and Batya quietly stood and left. Mara saw them out and then returned to Simon.

"I am going to sleep. Are you coming?"

He patted her hand. "I think I will stay up here awhile longer."

Mara leaned down and kissed his cheek, and then she quietly descended the steps back to the main floor.

Simon lay on the rooftop for a long while, pondering the evening's conversation. He decided the time had come. He needed to know if he would truly leave everything to follow the Messiah. He was fearful that he would discover he was not willing. But even more concerning to him was the thought of not knowing.

27

The following evening after Mara and Simon had cleaned up their meal and said evening prayers with their three younger children, Simon asked Mara to follow him to the roof.

"Sit with me," he said when they got there.

"You seem excited."

"I am, Mara. While I believe I have been following Jesus this past year, it's always been from a distance. I feel I am so close, but so close is not enough. I need to *know*. If Jesus is telling the truth, if he is truly the Son of God, if his new commandments are truly how we must live, then I believe it's vital for me to find out for myself. And I know that if I ask God, he will show me the way."

Mara just smiled at him. "You *know* that? How long have you known that?"

Simon mused, "For much longer than I wish to admit. A few years ago, when I first found Alexander in Capernaum, he told me about the day Jesus taught on the mountainside. I felt something very strongly then, and I prayed that night for God to tell me if he would answer my questions. He told me, beyond any doubt, that he would."

She looked confused. "That was a few years ago? And you are only now beginning to ask?"

Simon looked at her sadly. "I know. It seems to make no sense. For the longest time I have been afraid."

"Afraid? Really? I have always felt you were afraid of nothing," Mara said.

"I was afraid I was not the kind of man who would give up everything, like you said you would. When I received the knowledge that God *would* answer me, I was afraid of what I would hear when I asked—not what I'd learn about Jesus but what I'd learn about myself."

She grabbed his hands.

"My sweet, honorable husband, I want you to know how happy this makes me. What do you think has changed in you?"

Simon smiled and said, "Do you mean besides that I am no longer a stubborn man?"

"Oh, I don't think that has changed."

They both laughed.

"No, I suppose it hasn't, and it is probably why this has taken so long. I think what has changed is that all along, even though I have loved his teachings, I have believed it is all up to me. Mara, I have tried hard to be the kind of man I felt I needed to be . . ."

"And you have, Simon. No woman could be more fortunate."

"But I have always felt everything was on me. I think I have not allowed God to work his miracles in my life. And now I understand that this has actually shown him I don't trust him."

"Really, Simon? I would never say that you don't trust God."

He squeezed her hands again in appreciation. "I know. I

wouldn't have either until now. But I think that's really what it is." He thought, and his face lit up. "If I took Samuel and put him up on a wall, and put out my arms, asking him to jump to me, but instead he climbed down carefully, he would be acting responsibly, but he would not be trusting me that there was a better way. He found one answer, but there was a better answer, and until he trusted me, he would not be able to find it."

Mara continued to watch him, saying nothing.

"I think God has been trying for a long time to teach me to trust him. He gave me you—someone who needs so much less proof to believe in him—as an example. But . . ." Simon's eyes filled with tears.

"But he has not given up on me, stubborn as I am. I am in awe of how much I think he loves me. I need to do my best to know if I can completely love and follow him. To trust him. To give up everything if he asks me to."

They each leaned forward, putting their foreheads against one another and holding hands. He looked down at her hands tightly clasping his and saw one of her tears fall upon them.

"Mara, I need time alone to pray, to ask for help. I hope you will understand, but I would like to stay up here for a while by myself tonight."

She said nothing. She leaned forward and took his cheeks in her hands and kissed him on the forehead. She then stood, walked quietly to the steps, and went down.

Simon sat for quite some time, looking up at the evening sky. He had contemplated for a long time how to address God but was still not sure he knew how. Sitting cross-legged, he placed his elbows on his knees and clasped his hands. He spoke out loud.

"Adonay, I am not sure I really know how to pray to you the right way."

He thought of all the prayers he had uttered in his life—real, true heartfelt prayers. He was ashamed there were so few he could remember most of them. Most clear to him was the first, the one he had uttered as he leaned against his house, terrified that Mara was in danger during Alexander's birth. He remembered the relief that came almost instantly after saying amen, when he heard Alexander cry, followed by the calming voice of the midwife. Then something struck him. He put his head down.

"Dear Adonay, I don't think I ever thanked you for blessing Mara and Alexander. I'm sorry. Thank you for saving my wife and son."

He felt a peace move through him as though someone had placed a warm cloak over him on a cold evening.

He looked up at the sky again, and he felt contentment. He felt happy he had remembered to do that, to say thank you, and it felt right. He also realized something so surely it startled him. His eyes opened wide as he looked at the stars. God had heard his prayer then, years ago, and he was hearing this one; and in his way, he had just answered Simon. He realized that God was waiting, right now this very evening, this moment, and he was ready to listen, and most amazingly, ready to answer whatever Simon asked him.

Simon changed his position to be on his knees. He clasped his hands in front of him, bowed his head, and began to speak. He did not know if this was the proper way to pray, but he did know for sure that this way would be acceptable before God. He had intended to ask God a question, but instead he started telling God everything that had happened in his life these last several years. He explained to him the things that had upset him and confused him. As he did, mistakes he had made toward others came to mind, and he asked for God's forgiveness, promising that if he found himself in those situations again, he would try to act differently. He told him the things that had touched his heart, the fears he had felt. The more Simon spoke, the more comfortable he became sharing everything, and the closer he felt to God. At times he cried in regret, and others in awe. Now and then he would stop speaking and feel a comfortable, perfect peace as he waited for more thoughts to flow into his mind and heart.

He never noticed the few times Mara quietly ascended the steps to check on him, heard him speaking, and then hurried back down to their room to afford Simon his privacy. He had no idea that down in their room, Mara was offering up her own prayers to God, pleading for him to hear Simon and answer him. He could not know that several houses away, Rufus could not sleep and had felt compelled to pray in behalf of his father. Or that hundreds of miles away, Alexander too was awake in the middle of the night, overcome with a peaceful urgency to pray for Simon. All Simon knew was that, for the first time in his life, he felt he was speaking with God and that whatever came of it, this was the right thing to do.

Simon also had no sense of the night's passage.

When he lifted his head and wiped his eyes dry, he was

surprised to see a faint lightening on the horizon, bearing witness to the coming dawn.

He bowed his head and spoke again. "God I am committing myself to thee. I want to be your disciple. I am not sure I can be all you need me to be, but I would like to try. Please help me to know if I am worthy to be called your disciple."

Simon took a deep breath and lay back on the mat. As he watched the sky lighten, he did not know what would happen, but he knew he had done what he needed to do. He knew—in fact, he was certain—that the answer would come, in God's way, when God was ready.

28

Simon slept briefly, from the first signs of dawn until sunrise. Despite the short rest, when he awoke he was full of energy. He stood and surveyed the view. He had seen it countless times before; but somehow today it felt new to him. Miles away, the water sparkled in the morning light. The sky was a beautiful vibrant blue with faint streaks of white. He was overcome with the beauty of it all. *How have I never noticed this before, in this way?* he wondered.

He walked down the steps, anxious to find Mara and share his experience. As he came toward their room, he heard the voices of Rufus and his family. He walked into their dining area and looked at Mara. They spoke not a word. Instead, his smile told her everything she wanted to hear. She walked quickly to him and threw her arms around his neck.

"Good morning," he said.

She hugged him harder.

Finally they ended their embrace and turned toward the table. Rufus's children began to giggle.

"Well, good morning to both of you!" Rufus said.

Simon walked Mara to the table. "What brings you here so early?" he asked, holding Mara's hand tight.

"Father, I had to come over. I was praying for you last night and had a thought. Passover is coming soon, and I wondered if you—all of you, actually—would like to travel to go find the Messiah and hear him speak."

Something leapt in Simon's heart. He almost had to laugh at himself, thinking about the earlier invitation from Alexander and how he'd held himself back. Now he could hardly contain himself.

"Yes! I would love to hear him." He looked at his children. "I think it would be wonderful for all the family to hear him."

He then looked right at Rufus and said, "I am ready to hear him."

Rufus nodded. "Wonderful!" he said. "I have work to do at the shop today. Let me complete that, but I think if we leave tomorrow, we should be able to get to Jerusalem in plenty of time. If Jesus is not there, I don't believe he'll be far."

All the children started to speak at once. "Can we see Alexander and Devorah and Esther and Chava?"

In all these years, Simon had never taken his whole family to any of the regions where he'd done so much of his work. They would indeed try to see Alexander. *But to hear the Messiah!* Simon had thought of nothing else from the moment Rufus mentioned it.

Everyone was furiously busy the rest of the day. They packed clothing, prepared food for the journey, and made provisions for their animals.

Just as dawn broke the following day, Rufus and his family arrived at Simon's home. They had secured the services of a man with two camels who would carry their things to the shore. Though the walk to port would take a half day, it would be mostly downhill.

Once they arrived, the children would be tired, but they would have several days aboard ship to rest.

With Passover coming, Simon's family was not the only one hoping to make the pilgrimage to Jerusalem. Throngs of people crowded the docks, some clearly new to the process of securing passage and negotiating fares with Roman ship captains. Simon told his family to sit and rest for a while. Then he began walking the harbor, a silent prayer in his heart that he would find someone with enough room to take the nine of them together.

He scanned the row of boats tied to the docks and glanced at the smattering of larger ships waiting at buoys just off shore for a space to unload and reload. He saw another, a little farther out, making its approach to the harbor. This ship caught his attention for some reason, but he couldn't quite figure out why.

Just then, Simon noticed that the boat in the very last slip along the dock was casting off. He watched as it slowly negotiated its way out into the channel and headed to sea. The ship that had caught his attention earlier then began to turn ever so slightly, clearly maneuvering toward the newly available slip. In an instant, realization dawned upon him. Soon, Simon was visibly beaming as he watched the ship's captain—teenage son by his side—carefully dock the boat and call on his crew to secure the lines.

Simon grinned as he walked toward the new arrival, his hands waving greetings in the air. The captain stared at him for a few moments, then burst into a smile of recognition and began waving back.

"My friend!" the captain shouted as he disembarked. "I thought we might cross paths again sometime."

"You recognized me . . ."

"Of course," the captain said as he stepped closer. "I told you I would pray for you, pray that you would find what you asked for. I have done so. Have you found your answers?"

Simon smiled.

"All of it and more," he said. "I have my family with me, and we are going to Judea. We want to find the Messiah and hear him teach."

The captain turned his head toward the sea and rubbed his beard.

Simon could only see the captain's profile but could tell he'd blinked his eyes a few times before turning back to face Simon.

"Then my prayers are answered as well," the captain said as he took a breath. "I suppose you are looking for passage. How many of you are there?"

"Nine."

The captain turned toward his son, who had followed him off the ship, and they spoke briefly.

"It will be a bit tight, but since you already all know each other, I suppose that will be acceptable to you?"

Simon shook the captain's hand vigorously. "That will be just fine. Let me get them."

Simon alternated between a fast walk and a run as he hurried back down the wharf, looking for his family. He found them sitting under a tree and excitedly told them about finding the captain. He had been concerned that they might have to split into two groups to find passage, but those worries vanished. Rufus stood and picked up as many of their bundles as he could.

"So, Father, the Lord provides," Rufus said.

"He does, he does. Everyone, follow me."

They carried their things back to the ship. When the captain saw them, he called to his son, who hurried over to help. The boy quickly went to Simon's eldest daughter, Miriam, and smiled at her as he offered to take her shoulder bag. But just as the boy put out his arms, Simon handed him his own, heavier bag. The quick glance that took place between the two youths just then was not lost on Simon, nor was the momentary look of scorn Miriam offered him.

Once aboard, they arranged places to sit while the captain and his crew finished loading cargo. The prevailing winds usually blew from west to east, which would favor the little group on their journey. If the weather was calm, they would be in Joppa in five to six days. The captain would likely stop two or three times to transfer cargo, but since Simon and his family took up all the available passenger room, each porting would be fast.

It was a smooth trip, and the days passed quickly as the little family spent time watching the shoreline, resting, and sharing their thoughts and excitement about seeing the Messiah. Several times, the captain and Simon removed themselves to a corner of the deck where Simon shared everything that had happened to him.

Upon arriving in Joppa, Rufus set out to learn if anyone knew where Jesus was preaching, and Simon worked to secure donkeys for the trip. He wanted to cover as much ground as possible, so he purchased six of the animals to carry their things and to allow for the younger members of the family, along with Mara and Batya on occasion, to ride as much as possible.

As Simon was completing the transaction, Rufus came running to him with excitement.

"Father, I found a man who came from Jerusalem this morning. He said that just two days ago Jesus came with his apostles to the city."

"Wonderful! We can make it there by tomorrow evening."

Simon called to Mara. "Can you and Batya get us two days' worth of food? Children! Help me load up our new family members."

The children excitedly stroked the donkeys, naming each one.

As he worked alongside his father, Rufus shared what he'd learned. "Father, this man said there are great crowds. As Jesus entered the city riding on a donkey, his followers laid palms before him and openly proclaimed him the Son of David and the promised Messiah. They speak boldly of this now."

Simon smiled at his son.

"We have come at a good time," he said. "We will get there a few days before Passover. I cannot think of a better time to hear him."

Rufus then looked somewhat subdued. "This man also said that Jesus is preparing to take over the armies."

Simon stopped adjusting the loads. "Is this what the prophecy says?"

Rufus looked concerned. "It does, but I don't think in the way this man thinks. I'm not sure how many share his thoughts . . . or what they might do when the Messiah does not do what they expect."

Simon returned to his work.

"Let's talk as we walk," he told his son. "Whatever happens, I want to get there as quickly as we can."

Simon left the final preparations to Rufus and went in search of a caravan to join. The city was teeming with people, and there would likely be almost one continuous stream of travelers making the trip. He found a group that looked nearly ready to leave, and ran back to his family to tell them.

As he began to lead them over to where the caravan members were assembling, he looked at Mara. Something overcame him. Tears filled his eyes, and he hugged her and kissed her.

"What was that for?" she asked.

"I'm not sure. I am just happy we are on this journey together."

Moments later, the first of the caravan began moving. Simon waited until he could blend into the middle and then walked his family and their train of animals into the mass flowing forward.

❖   ❖   ❖

The first day of travel was uneventful. It seemed everyone was going the same direction, which was not surprising given the coming of Passover only a few days hence. On the second day, however, as they drew closer, they began to pass an occasional group traveling the other direction. When that happened, everyone in Simon's caravan would stop and press the other group for information.

It was at the end of that day when the news of the temple came.

29

A large crowd had gathered around the fire; they were urging the man to tell his story one more time.

He began again. "It was the morning after he rode into Jerusalem. He had come to the temple. And he saw just what he had three years ago—money changers set up in within the temple walls. He began to overturn their tables, and he chased them out, chastising them."

Someone from the crowd called out, "What did he say?"

"He said they had made the temple a den of thieves."

"But then," the man continued, "he invited we who had witnessed it to come and sit by him. And he taught us! And then many started bringing their loved ones who were blind or lame to him. One by one, the Messiah healed them all."

When the man finished talking, and the larger group of listeners began to disperse, a smaller group gathering closer together to ask the traveler more questions. Simon and Rufus walked forward so they could hear.

"How did the Sanhedrin react?" one man asked.

"They are not happy," the man answered warily. "They had representatives at the temple, and I watched them as Jesus cleared the court. You would think they would be pleased he was honoring the temple, but they were visibly upset."

Another chimed in. "Why are they so bothered?"

The man looked his way and replied instantly: "He challenges their authority. They have said he blasphemes by calling himself the Son of God. Jesus outwardly blames them for allowing the temple to be defiled; and in so many other things, he suggests that their judgments are not in keeping with God's ways."

"Well," said another, "I think that's a good thing. They need to be challenged. We complain so much about Rome, but the Sanhedrin controls us as almost as much as Pilate does."

"Yes, but they will not settle for it," the traveler responded. "I have heard from others that they have had enough of Jesus and are plotting to kill him."

Several questioned him to find out if that could really be true; but Simon and Rufus stepped away.

"Father, do you feel safe continuing on? It seems the tensions are high."

Simon looked at the ground, his lips pursed. "Normally, Rufus, I'd say no. But I felt prompted to make this trip as soon as you suggested it. Let's be watchful, but let's continue. If either of us feels the family is in danger, we'll tell the other and decide what to do."

The following morning, as they packed their animals, it was with subdued excitement. Simon and Rufus quietly agreed that they should be watchful for those who might be traveling with the group as informants to the Sanhedrin. They advised the younger children to stay close, and Simon told Miriam to keep a more careful watch.

The pace was again slow, but Simon had traversed this road more times than he could count. He calculated that they would arrive in Jerusalem early in the afternoon. He had a friend in the city with a large home who he knew would be happy to take them in. They should be able to get all settled before Passover began that evening. As they continued without incident, the mood lightened. Simon could not stop thinking. He was going to hear Jesus! Hear his words in his own ears! For the first time, he would not have to rely on second- and thirdhand retellings. His children would remember this the rest of their lives and tell their children and grandchildren of this experience.

The caravan stopped in Emmaus for the travelers to replenish their food and water and to take their noonday meal.

As they set out one last time, Simon felt like a young child again. They had only just left when he heard an odd noise. Crossing over to the other side of the road, he looked ahead. There at the edge was a man not much older than his sons. Simon squinted at him to try to see what was wrong. As they got closer, he could hear the man calling out nonsensical words. Simon noticed that as each group walked past the man, they would appear to be deep in conversation and turn the other way, so as to avoid looking at him.

Simon pulled his lead donkey off to the side of the road to let others begin to pass.

"Wait here," was all he said to his family. As he walked up to the man, he noticed a terrible stench. He stood over him and realized the man must not have bathed in a long time. He did not appear to be poor, as his clothes were finer than would be the case if that were true. But Simon could also smell the strong odor of wine. The man was intoxicated. Simon stood looking at him, not sure what to do, when another member of the caravan walked up to him.

"I have seen him before," the man told Simon. "He lives in Emmaus. He is always drunk. Be glad he is not able to walk today. Most of the time he accosts those who pass through the town." The man then spat toward the drunken man and kept walking.

Simon had seen many men like this in his years of traveling. And though he would never have spit upon them, he had always kept his distance. He had also always felt strongly that each man must be responsible for himself and that he did not have to be involved in another's poor decisions.

Until now.

He gazed down at the man, who still hadn't seemed to notice Simon. The man kept uttering senseless words, his eyes closed. Simon wanted to turn away, but something stronger than his own feelings drew him to the man. Almost without knowing why, Simon squatted down next to him. While it was difficult to do, between the smell of wine and vomit and human filth, Simon put out his hand and touched the man's shoulder. Slowly, deliberately, the drunken man turned his head toward Simon.

"What is your name?" Simon asked. The man tried to reply, but it was garbled. After repeated tries, Simon was finally able to discern that the man was saying "Daniel."

"Daniel," Simon asked, "where is your family? Are they in Emmaus?" He overpronounced every word to get the man's attention.

"No," Daniel spit out. "Bethen."

Simon tried to repeat it back to him. "Bethany?"

Again, Daniel shook his head. Loudly, he said, "Bethem!"

"Bethlehem?" Simon asked back.

Daniel nodded and lay down. Simon stood and walked to his family. They gathered around him. "I assumed his family was in Emmaus, and I thought we could wait while I took him back there. But he says they are in Bethlehem. I . . ."

Simon looked back at the man. Then he turned to his family and said, "I don't know what will happen to him if we ignore him. We need to get to Jerusalem; but I can't leave him."

He watched their faces. The children looked disappointed, and the youngest seemed frightened as they looked toward Daniel. But Rufus caught Simon's eye and smiled. Simon turned to Mara.

"Mara, I . . ."

She drew closer to him and squeezed his hand. "We will be fine. Rufus will be with us."

Simon nodded. He turned and looked toward Jerusalem, which had recently come into view on the far horizon.

"Rufus, take everyone there. There is man named Eber, a friend Alexander and I have stayed with many times. We are a large group, but he has a large home and is a good man, and I know he will allow all of you in."

Simon explained how to find the man's home and then said, "I will take one of the donkeys and get Daniel to Bethlehem—find his family. It's a small town, so it should not take me long. I will try to get back tonight, but at the latest, I will find you in the morning."

"You will be traveling on Passover," Rufus said.

"I know," Simon replied, "and that is not ideal. But I don't think Daniel's problems will wait because it is Passover. I think God will understand."

Rufus smiled. "I know he will. God be with you, Father. We will see you tonight or tomorrow."

Simon kissed each of his family and embraced Mara, who gave him a long hug. She came up on her tiptoes and whispered in his ear. "I don't think I have ever been prouder of my husband."

He smiled at her and said, "Pride is a sin, Mara."

She patted his cheek. "Not this kind. God be with you."

Rufus then helped Simon move their things off one of the donkeys and fashioned a seat for Daniel on the beast. They lifted Daniel onto the donkey, forced him to lean forward, and then secured him so he would not fall. Simon took a flask of water and offered it to Daniel, who could not lift it but managed to drink part of the water that flowed from it, the rest spilling to the ground.

Simon's family returned to the caravan, this time near its rear. They turned back frequently to look at him as they walked, waving until they could no longer see him. Simon also waved until they were out of sight.

"All right, Daniel, let's go," he finally said. "Let's find your family."

They turned and walked back toward Emmaus until Simon found the road to Bethlehem.

30

Simon had not anticipated how slow going this trip would be. Because Daniel was not as tightly secured as Simon had intended, the only travel arrangement that seemed to work forced Simon to walk right by the donkey's side, his hand on Daniel's back in case he slipped one way or the other.

Several times, the rocking of the donkey made Daniel ill, and he would vomit. Simon stopped whenever this happened and allowed Daniel to finish. Then he'd take water and the edge of his cloak and clean Daniel's face. Many travelers passed them. Some would stare; others would turn in disgust or say something demeaning. Not one stopped to ask if they could help. Simon did not blame them. He had to admit that the whole experience was unsettling, but he was nonetheless singular in his purpose.

As the afternoon wore on, Daniel slowly became more coherent. At first he would just look at Simon and then put his head back down. But later, as the sun began to set, he spoke his first word.

"Why?"

It startled Simon at first; he had not heard anyone speak for hours.

"Why, what?" Simon responded.

Daniel was barely able to form a sentence. "Why you doing this?"

Simon stared at Daniel for a moment, then said, "Because you need it."

Daniel looked like he was going to be ill again, but he took a big breath and managed to speak. "I don't want to go to Bethlehem."

Simon laughed. "That would have been a good thing to tell me earlier in the day. At this point, Daniel, you are going to Bethlehem. We will find your family and then, if you want to leave again, that's up to you."

Daniel looked away. Eventually he said, "My family will not want to see me."

Simon looked at him and asked, "Why not? It's your family."

"Seeing me like this," Daniel said, his faced still turned away, "they will not want me there. My family keeps the laws. This will embarrass them."

Simon listened and then challenged him: "How do you know? Have they seen you like this before?"

Daniel shook his head. "They have not seen me at all."

"For how long?" Simon asked.

Daniel did not answer. It didn't seem like he was trying to figure out how many years had passed. Rather, it seemed he did not want to say.

Finally, Daniel said quietly, "Since I was a younger man."

Simon walked on without a word. He honestly did not know how this man's family would react. And he also did not know what he would do if they wouldn't take Daniel in. *What if it has been so long they do not even live there anymore?* Simon wondered. But he pushed the thought out of his mind, remaining sure of only one thing: he needed to get this man to Bethlehem.

Eventually they reached the outskirts of town, and Simon stopped.

"Let's get you straightened up," he said as he took off the man's outer robe and wet it a little. He wiped Daniel's face again and tried to clean his hair a bit. Simon looked at the robe, sighed, and then threw it into a trench by the side of the road. He then took off his own cloak and put it around Daniel.

"That will have to do. Now, can you tell me where your family lives?"

Daniel pointed, and Simon again led the donkey.

They entered Bethlehem, Daniel directing them at each intersection with a nod of his head until, finally, he looked toward a door. Simon stopped.

He looked carefully at the home, staring at the door. "This is your family's home?"

Daniel nodded, a look of sadness—and fear—in his eyes.

Under his breath, Simon whispered, "I know this place."

He helped Daniel off the donkey and placed the stumbling man's left arm around his own shoulders. Daniel could support his own weight but could not balance himself at all, so Simon simply left the donkey standing in the road and approached the door, steadying Daniel with both hands around his waist as they walked. His stomach tightened when they reached the door, but he took a deep breath . . . and knocked.

In a few moments, a man opened the door. He was tall, husky, aged, and though more than thirty years had passed, Simon recognized him instantly. The man looked at Simon as though he might recognize him as well. His gaze then turned to Daniel; and revulsion moved across his face. Simon said nothing. After only a few seconds, the man's eyes widened. He bent over, looking more closely. Suddenly, tears filled his eyes, and all he could say was, "My son."

The man took Daniel in his arms and walked him into their home. Soon the man's wife came, crying out her son's name between sobs. They all three fell to the floor, Daniel leaning against his father, and his mother stroking his hair. They rocked back and forth over and over again. Simon saw Daniel's body start to shake as he cried, his arms wrapped tight around both of his parents.

Simon knew they had forgotten him, and that was fine with him. Smiling, he quietly pulled the door closed, then walked outside to his donkey, patted its head, and took up the reins.

"You did well, my friend. Thank you for helping me."

Just as he was about to start walking, he felt a strong but gentle hand clasp his shoulder. He turned to face the elderly man. The father was still emotional, struggling to get words out. "I know you."

Simon smiled at him. "And I you."

"You found my son. What made you help him?"

"Well, a very long time ago, a good man in this very house told me that it did not matter where we were, only that we might help someone on their journey."

The householder smiled at him and said, "You must come in and stay with us."

"My family has gone to Jerusalem for Passover," Simon told him. "I need to go meet them."

The man looked worried. "Not this late at night. Stay here and go in the morning. We would like you to eat with us."

Simon looked at the sky. He had not realized how late it was. He felt a wave of exhaustion come over him, and sighed. "I think I will. Thank you."

The man walked Simon and the donkey around the back. "You go in. I will tend to your animal."

Simon thanked him and walked in the back door of their home. The man's wife had already helped Daniel change his clothes, and though his appearance still needed a bit more work, he looked much cleaner than before. He looked at Simon and said nothing but offered a small, tired smile and bowed his head toward him. Simon smiled and walked to sit at the table, patting Daniel on the back as he passed him.

Eventually, the table was set with enough food to feed several times more than the four who sat around it. Daniel did not speak, but he looked content. His mother sat next to him, helping him eat.

After a quiet period of eating, the father looked at Simon. "My friend, I am still bold," he said, "so I yearn to ask you: Did you find the reason you were here all those years ago?"

Simon stopped eating. The span of the past thirty-three years hit him. Just feet from where they now sat, this good man had challenged him to find out why he had been led to Bethlehem on that sacred night. And here, sitting with these good people, he knew the answer without a doubt.

"I did," was all he could say through an emotional smile.

For most of the meal, Simon shared the details of his spiritual journey over the last three decades.

When the conversation slowed, the father looked at him. "There is no way we can ever thank you. All I can tell you is my family will bless your name forever."

Simon looked off toward the door and then turned back to the man. "I think I will walk for a while. It's been a long day, and this was a wonderful meal. I would like to get started early tomorrow, but I'll sleep better if I go out for a bit."

"Would you like company?" the man asked.

"I think I need to be alone with my thoughts, and I think your family needs time together. I won't be long."

Simon stood, but before he could leave, Daniel's mother ran to him and hugged him. She tried to speak but gave up and hugged Simon again. Finally, she stood back and said, "Give that to your family to thank them for letting you save my son."

"I will," Simon smiled and then went out the door.

When Simon stepped out, he immediately turned toward the edge of town. Though Bethlehem had changed somewhat, he was sure he would recognize the spot he was looking for.

When he reached the edge of the village, he turned and began to walk through the fields. He saw herds of sheep with shepherds, some old, some young, standing in their midst. Occasionally a sheep would look at him, sense no worry, and look down again, continuing to eat. Simon smiled, and the thought came to him that many of these shepherds had not even been born the last time he walked out here. He looked at the ridge to his right, watching each cave as he passed. Like that night long ago, there were travelers occupying many of the spots tonight due to the crowds in Jerusalem.

Finally, Simon stopped. He looked closely at the outcroppings and decided this was the cave. He peered in carefully and noticed in the moonlight that only a few sheep lay inside. He walked toward the opening. At first he wanted to walk in, but then he felt more comfortable sitting on a rock at the entrance. He looked at the empty ground before him, remembering how the shepherds had stood and knelt that night as they watched the young family inside. He closed his eyes, remembering the feelings of peace—feelings he could not identify at the time but that he now understood well. He played each sound and smell and sight over and over in his mind.

Suddenly he recalled another feeling, one that made him less comfortable. Guilt.

On that night thirty-three years ago, the couple and their new babe were here, in a cave, because he had been unwilling to give up his room. How could he have been so selfish? Even if Mary had been nothing but a commoner, his act would have been considered shameful. But he had denied a room for the birth of the Son of God! Suddenly the horror of his place in history tore through his soul. Simon looked around at the cave, the cave he had sentenced the little family to, and then he looked at the ground and began to cry. In the solitude of the cave, he let go of the emotions he had carried all these years: his worries about his family, his concerns about his own beliefs, his guilt from that night. It all came tumbling out of him in racking sobs, full-throated wails, and exclamations of sorrow and regret. Then, in the peace of that little hollow of land, all that pain simply dissipated into the cool evening air, gone for good.

After a period of time, Simon raised his head. He did not know how long he had been there, but he felt cleansed.

Then it hit him. That baby, now the Messiah, was just up the road in Jerusalem! Simon would find him and find some way to speak with him. He wanted to tell him how sorry he was. He knew he could never make it up to him, but he vowed he would find a way to help him, to do whatever was needed, no matter how menial, to spread his word—his gospel—far and wide.

Simon had never been filled with more purpose, more peace, more clarity than at that moment. He stood with renewed vigor and walked determinedly through the fields back to the home.

31

Early the next morning, Simon opened his eyes and was struck by a ray of brilliant sunlight streaming in through the eastern window. As he sat up and stretched his arms, he realized that—in addition to the sun—quite a bit of noise seemed to be coming from outside. As he opened the door and stepped out into the yard to take a look, he immediately sensed something was wrong.

People were talking anxiously everywhere. Many were crying; he could hear the sobbing of both women and men above the din of it all. He went in search of the householder and found him shortly.

"What is it?" he asked with trepidation as he grabbed the man's arm.

The man turned to him, a look of shock on his face. "A runner has just come from Jerusalem. They put Jesus on trial this morning."

"Trial?" Simon questioned. "On what charge?"

"Treason," he responded.

"Who? How could they do that?"

"I'm unsure. It seems either Pilate, or Herod Antipas, or both.

But the Sanhedrin were behind it, and"—he paused—"they've convicted him."

"What? What will happen to him?"

The man shook his head, unable to speak the words. Finally, he just said, "Crucifixion."

"When?"

"Today."

Simon immediately turned and started to run. The man called after him. "Your donkey . . ."

But Simon ignored him. The donkey could never move as fast he needed to. He grabbed his shoulder bag from the house and began running to Jerusalem.

32

Simon ran until his lungs hurt. And then he ran some more. He stubbed his feet on stones, tripping again and again. Soon his hands were bloodied from falling on the path so many times. He passed many travelers coming from the other direction, and their tear-stained faces searched his, hoping to find solace in a stranger. He hurried on. As he came to the steeper parts of the road, he walked quickly, then ran again as the path flattened out.

He was covered in sweat, his feet bleeding, but he felt none of it. When he finally reached the city gate, he stopped. He looked around, unsure what to do next. But then he saw Rufus.

"Father! I knew you would come up from Bethlehem as soon as you heard. I sent Mother and Batya and the children back to Eber's home, where we stayed, and I have been here waiting for you since it was announced."

Simon's face showed his horror. "Is it really true? They are crucifying him?"

Rufus tried to speak through his tears. "It is. Even Pilate tried to convince the people to release him using Passover tradition, but the people called for a murderer to be set free instead. I couldn't believe it! The crowd has lost its mind. People thought he would free them, take down the government, as we had heard, and then when he did not . . ."

"Where is he?" Simon interrupted.

"Hurry, follow me."

The men ran through the streets, pushing aside those in their way. Some hurled epithets at them, but they didn't notice. Soon Simon could hear the crowd, its noise growing louder and louder.

As they pushed their way between the hordes of people, Simon kept thinking that he must speak to Jesus. He must tell him he was sorry, that he would serve him and never again pass someone in need.

As they drew closer, the noise seemed more organized. The crowd was chanting! Simon could not believe what he heard. With bloodthirsty enthusiasm, the voices rose. "Crucify him! Crucify him!"

Tears filled Simon's eyes; anger filled his heart. He looked from left to right at the faces of the yelling people. They were like animals, lost in their demonic chants. Many were throwing their fists in the air with each syllable. Simon looked with fierceness at several of them, but he could not catch anyone's gaze. He felt as if he might explode and wished to swing his fists at everyone around him, screaming at those calling for the torture of the one who had come to save them. But then he heard his son's voice. It was soft but somehow louder than anything around them.

"Father," Rufus said calmly. "It's not his way. We must live as he taught, even here, right to the end. This is what he would want from us."

Simon looked hard at his son. He knew Rufus was right, and

he wanted to hold fast to the strength he offered. Finally, he nodded.

Through his tears, Rufus said to his father, "Come. Let's keep moving forward."

As they moved through the crowd, Simon no longer shoved everyone in his path. Instead, he firmly but gently moved those in front of him aside. He offered apologies, but nobody seemed to hear him. Except one, who turned toward him. It was an elderly woman. She was crying so hard she could not breathe and was panicking as the crowd pressed against her. Simon put both arms around her and pulled her close.

The woman clasped Simon's arm hard, saying again and again, "Why?"

He gently turned her in the direction he was going and said, "Come with me. We will see him together."

He kept his arm protectively around her and moved her through the crowd with him, going only as fast as she was able. Rufus helped support her from the other side.

Finally, the three of them found themselves at the front of the crowd. Twenty paces before them was an archway leading into a large palace. Everyone stared intently at the opening, chanting and waiting. Then, those on the other side of the roadway who could see through the doorway began cheering. A change traveled through the crowd like a wave.

A few Roman soldiers stepped out, snapping their whips.

Simon stopped breathing.

A man walked slowly behind the soldiers. His robes were tattered and blood-stained. The rips in his garments revealed gaping wounds. On his head, a circle of thorny vines pressed into his scalp, fresh blood dripping from the marks it left. He was unsteady on his feet, and he looked forward as though he saw no one.

This was Jesus, the Messiah, the Son of God.

Simon looked to the ground and noticed a heavy beam. It was as long as a man was tall and too thick to put both hands around. He grew nauseated, remembering the one crucifixion he had seen before. He knew what was coming.

He held the old woman closer as she brought her hands to her mouth. Rufus grabbed Simon's arm but stood tall. Somehow, though they could not stop what was happening, they both knew they needed to be here. If nothing else, they needed their reverent silence to bear witness of the Son of God, and they needed to stand in contrast to those who sought his demise.

The guard grabbed the shoulder of Jesus's robe and pointed down at the beam with his other hand. Jesus slowly bent over, reaching for the beam, but there was little chance he would be able to lift the heavy wood that would become part of the cross.

The guard watched momentarily and then, shaking his head in frustration, looked into the crowd.

Simon knew exactly what the guard was searching for, and he knew exactly what he must do.

Everything stopped in that moment. Simon saw parts of his life in review: the table at the inn with its view of the door, the evening walk by the cave so many years ago, the stories he had heard through the intervening years, the fear he'd later felt when he thought he could lose his son over these stories. He recalled how he had changed since then. It somehow seemed a distant memory, something from another time, another life. How he was now was his reality. A small smile came to his lips. He knew what was about to happen, and he knew, beyond any doubt whatsoever, what he was willing to do. God was answering his prayer in the way and time that was right for Simon.

He did not leap out or try to seek the guard's attention. Simon knew with certainty that as the guard scanned the crowd, he would meet Simon's eyes and stop him. He would demand Simon step out of the crowd, pick up the cross, and carry it. He would threaten Simon with the whip, but Simon would feel no fear. Not because he knew he wouldn't be hurt but because it didn't matter. This God before him was his Savior, and Simon knew with perfect clarity that if he was called to die for him, he would.

He slowly removed the woman's hands from his arm and stood tall. The guard looked his way, and their eyes locked.

"You!" the guard yelled at him. "Get out here!"

Rufus started to hold Simon back, but Simon gently pushed him off. He walked forward, never releasing his gaze from the guard, who looked increasingly confused.

"What is your name?" the guard demanded.

Simon looked squarely at him and proclaimed, "I am Simon, of Cyrene."

"Well, Simon of Cyrene, pick up that beam and carry it. Now!"

Simon stepped over the crossbar so that he was facing up the hill. He attempted to lift the wood but struggled. Another guard stepped out at the first guard's orders and held the beam up at an angle while Simon squatted down and lifted it across the back of his shoulders. Immediately, he felt sharp splinters dig into his skin. He bent his head down so that the beam would could rest across his back. The other guard stepped forward and leveled it some while Simon sat momentarily on his haunches, gathering the strength to stand.

His arms were extended out to each side, his hands balancing the incredible weight. He focused on his legs and then, with more will than strength, pushed against his thighs and calves. Slowly he started rising. He kept pushing and pushing. His legs burned. He did not think he was strong enough, but never for a second did he allow himself to consider anything but succeeding. Finally, his legs were straight, and he stepped a little to each side to widen his stance and steady himself.

The guards kept their hands on the beam until it appeared Simon was balanced, and then they slowly let go. Simon looked to his left at the guard who had summoned him out. The guard motioned with his head for Simon to begin walking. Simon looked in the guard's eyes and saw a man who was somehow different from the exasperated one who just moments ago demanded Simon take up this task. He saw a man who did not want to be doing this but was bound by duty. He saw a man who was working to keep his personal feelings at bay. And he saw a man who looked upon him, Simon, with a small dose of admiration. Simon looked to his right and saw Rufus, who now held the old woman. He smiled faintly at his son through his tears and began to walk.

Simon was not sure how long it took. His mind seemed to fade in and out of awareness of his surroundings. Most of the crowd was focused on the Messiah, who walked ahead of him but whom Simon couldn't see, for he was forced to keep his head down so that his shoulders could hold the cross. But as he looked at the ground, he could see drops of blood trailing in front of him, letting him know he was still following his Master. Something pulsed through him, giving him strength and purpose.

Suddenly he felt the beam lighten, and it seemed to float off his shoulders. Through hazy vision, he saw the colors of Roman uniforms on either side of him lift the beam over his head and carry it away. Another guard shoved him off to the side; he tripped but was supported by a strong grasp. The arms that caught him lifted him up gently and then pulled him in close.

"Father, it's Alexander. I've got you."

Simon reached up, put his hand on Alexander's arm, and then blacked out.

33

Simon felt a cool cloth on his forehead. He opened his eyes and tried to focus. After several blinks, he saw Mara's face close to his. She was crying silently, stroking his head. He put his arm around her and weakly pulled her close. He looked around and saw Alexander and Rufus there with him as well.

Simon then noticed that the day had become cloudy and dark. He looked past Mara to see dozens of people in front of him, crying and holding each other. There was no more chanting or yelling. He looked up toward the hill, and saw there, against the clouds, the silhouettes of three men—each hanging lifeless on a cross.

Mara pulled back from him, and Simon asked hoarsely, "Is it done?"

She nodded and began to cry again. Rufus and Alexander sat down next to them, their eyes fixed on the crosses atop the hill.

Without removing his gaze, Alexander said quietly, "When he died, the earth shook."

Simon stared. He could not remove his eyes from the scene on the hill. He tried to burn it into his memory, to never forget. He stared at the Messiah, taking in as many details of his appearance as possible in the waning light. He looked at the other two men, one on each side of Jesus, and saw their legs badly mangled. As he looked back to Jesus, he saw that despite the nails in his limbs and a wound at his side, his body hung unbroken. The Savior's head was down upon his chest. Simon could see, against the sky, the acute detail of the thorny crown that remained on his head. Simon looked because he had to. He must remember it exactly as he saw it.

In time, the crowd thinned, and the soldiers began unceremoniously taking down the bodies of the crucified, as if they were removing trash. A Jewish leader dressed in the robes of the Sanhedrin stood over the body of Jesus, watching the soldiers. When they had finished removing the nails, the man handed the soldiers a scroll. They looked at it, shrugged their shoulders, and allowed the leader to direct what appeared to be some of his servants to carry the body down a path and out of sight.

Alexander lifted his mother; Rufus slowly helped Simon to his feet.

"Come," Alexander said. "I think we should go back."

The four of them walked slowly down the hill from Golgotha.

34

The next day was the Sabbath. All of Jerusalem was in confusion. There were those who felt relief—glad this preoccupation with Jesus was finally over, that a political nightmare had come to an end. There were those who believed that the promises God had made them (since Abraham's time!) were now destroyed. And then there were those who were not sure what had happened but who knew that, somehow, God's purposes would continue to be fulfilled.

All of Simon's family—children and grandchildren—were gathered at Eber's home. Eber and his wife were also followers and quietly mourned with them. There was very little discussion between any of them because there was simply nothing to say. They could do little but turn the events of the previous day over and over in their minds.

For most of the day, Simon was silent. Mara attended to the wounds on his neck and hands, and he drifted in and out of sleep. His younger children took turns sitting by him, leaning close. He would periodically look at their faces and try to comfort them with a smile or a squeeze of the hand.

Near the end of the day, both Eber and Alexander ventured out for news. When they returned, they sat in the open courtyard by Simon and called the others to gather around.

"It is difficult to find the truth," Alexander began. "Speculation and rumor are everywhere. There are so many who wanted the crucifixion, and so we had to be careful who we spoke with. We did not feel safe around those who favored it."

"That Sanhedrin you saw," Eber said, "appears to be a man called Joseph. He comes from Arimathea, west of Jerusalem. People are saying that he did not support the sentencing and that he asked Pilate for the Master's body. Joseph is apparently a wealthy man and has a grand tomb in a garden near Golgotha. Joseph took him there and had him buried."

"What of the apostles?" Mara asked.

"We don't know," Alexander answered.

He paused and sighed deeply. "We could not find them. Perhaps they have gone into hiding for their own safety. There are so many followers, like us, who all seem to be wandering around trying to determine what to do. This is not what anyone expected."

No one offered anything else.

A short time later, as Simon's head became clearer, he noticed that Rufus, Alexander, and Mara had gone off by themselves to the roof. From his seat in the courtyard, Simon could see them quietly speaking. He stood, wincing at the pain he felt in his back and legs. And then, slowly, he straightened up and somewhat unsteadily crossed the courtyard and started up the steps to the roof. His sons noticed him as he came near the top and leapt up to grab his elbows, ushering him to a seat by Mara. After making sure he was comfortable, they sat down, and Rufus spoke.

"Father, this thing you did yesterday . . ."

Simon put up his hand immediately. "We will not speak of it."

"Let me just say this," Alexander interjected. "His followers, everywhere we went, were also speaking of you and what happened."

"Let it end there." Simon cut him off. "Trust me. We should speak of the Messiah. Nothing else."

Each of them sat quietly, unsure what to say. Finally, Alexander said, "I did not think it would end like this. I don't know what to do."

Simon sat up, more alert, but not without great pain.

"Why, Alexander, why don't you know what to do?"

Alexander looked at him with concern. "Father, I know you're recovering. You were passed out for hours yesterday at the foot of the cross. Do you not recall that he is dead? It's over."

Simon did not look at Alexander, nor did he answer the question. Instead, he looked out at the view of the city, finally saying, "Alexander, did you know your purpose three or four days ago?"

Alexander answered, "Of course. On those days, I was here in the city, and when I was not listening to Jesus, I was in the street teaching."

"Teaching what?" Simon asked.

Alexander spread his hands in confusion. "Teaching what the Savior taught. Sharing his new commandments and the promises he made if we follow them."

Simon turned back to them all. "And why wouldn't you

continue doing that today, and tomorrow, and the next and the next? Are his teachings no longer true?"

Alexander was quiet, breathing heavily as he pondered Simon's words.

When he didn't answer, Rufus spoke quietly. "Father, what *should* we do?"

Simon felt a great confidence fill him, his heart fairly burned in his chest. He surveyed the faces of his family, who had all patiently waited for him to come to accept Jesus as the promised Messiah. He looked at his two older boys, who had each bravely taken their places as devout disciples, teaching hundreds the messages of Jesus. They now looked to him to give them direction.

And he knew what to say.

"I am sad, as you are," Simon said warmly. "We will all never forget what we saw yesterday. But it is more important, so much more important, that you remember what we have felt and learned these last months and years."

He smiled. "All of you are so far ahead of me; you were so much more accepting of the truth when you heard it. But through your love and long-suffering with me, I too now believe."

Simon turned in the direction of the hill where Jesus had taken his last breaths. "Yesterday, as I stared at the cross, I tried to mark everything I saw in my memory. What kept coming to my mind were these words: 'Remember always, he overcomes all.'"

Simon looked back, his eyes on fire. "If what Jesus taught was true yesterday, then it will be true tomorrow. He is counting on us, each of us. What shall we do now? I am not sure but for this: I cannot hear what I have heard, and in caring for my fellow man, not go and share it. All I know is that as soon as I can, I will begin."

He slowly lifted his arm and put it around Mara.

She said only, "And I as well."

"And I," said Rufus.

"And I," said Alexander.

35

For the rest of the evening, the tone of the family's conversations changed. They were hushed and reverent in honor of what had transpired. But they spoke of ideas and plans and what they would do to carry the word forward.

When Simon awoke the next morning, he felt significantly better. He was sore, but he was able to stand up straight and walk without help.

Alexander and Rufus had left the house early to search for more information. When they did not return, Mara became worried. She did not speak of it, but Simon could tell. He walked close to her.

"They are safe. I feel sure of it."

Then, changing the topic, he said, "I'm going to get our animals ready. I think we can leave today."

Suddenly, everyone heard the door in the courtyard burst open. Alexander was yelling for the family, who gathered quickly in front of him. Tears were streaming down both his and Rufus's faces. Alexander tried to catch his breath. Without gathering his composure, he panted as he spoke.

"He is risen!"

36

The family erupted in joy and questions, crowding anxiously around the two men.

Simon, however, stood back from the group, his arms folded, and just watched his family. He quietly uttered a prayer of thanks for the Messiah and for this family of faithful men and women who loved God.

Mara noticed that her husband was not in the group and, finding him, walked over. With a big smile and through her own tears, she asked, "What do you think of all this?"

He just smiled and then softly said, "Let's talk later."

Alexander and Rufus had little information, but the family kept pressing them for more and more, and so they repeated what they knew.

Alexander began. "A woman called Mary—who has spent much time with Jesus and his apostles—and a few other women went to the tomb this morning to anoint the Lord's body. On the evening before the Sabbath, a large stone had been rolled in front of the tomb's entrance. The stone was so large it took several men to move it. Guards were posted in front of the stone to assure that no one could enter to steal or desecrate the body."

"But this morning," he continued, "when the women arrived, the guards were gone, and the stone had been moved. They went inside and discovered that his body was gone. As they mourned, a man appeared to them, seemingly out of nowhere. He told them that Jesus was not there because he was risen."

"How did the people who told you this learn of it?" Batya asked.

Alexander turned toward her. "Because this angel, which is what I suppose he was, told the women to get news of it to the disciples. When Peter heard the news, he ran to the tomb to see for himself. Word of it is now everywhere."

The group was quiet. They were all overcome with amazement, but most were asking themselves something else, something only their friend Eber had the courage to voice.

"You know I am a believer, but I have to ask, because I think the Sanhedrin will ask too: How do you know he is risen?"

Everyone turned to look at him.

"I mean," he continued, "how do we know that the women—who were surely emotional—did not make this up in an effort to explain what had happened to the body? How do we know that this 'angel' was not just a gardener who knew nothing and was playing them for fools?"

No one said anything.

Simon, who was seated on a rock at one side of the circle, began slowly pushing the end of a stick through the dirt at his feet. One by one, each family member heard the quiet motions of the stick. And, one by one, they turned toward Simon, suddenly knowing—somehow—that he would give them guidance.

Sensing everything around him, Simon looked up. His face was peaceful; there almost seemed to be a light emanating from him.

"We know he is risen," he said simply, "because he told us this would happen."

Everyone looked confused, but then Alexander's face suddenly showed understanding. He and Simon smiled at each other, and Simon continued.

"Alexander, remember when you told us how Jesus taught that we must take up our cross and follow him?"

"Of course," Alexander said quietly, his admiration for his father evident on his face.

"At the time, you also told us something he had said, that I think we have forgotten. You said he had told them he must go to Jerusalem to be tormented and suffer at the hands of the chief priests and others, to be killed, and then . . ."

Alexander interrupted, taking over from his father. "And then rise again on the third day!"

With a somewhat embarrassed look, he continued, "I don't suppose I really understood what he meant by *risen* at that time. I thought it must have been symbolic. After all, once someone is dead . . ."

He stopped and looked at his father, silently asking for more help.

Simon spoke softly. "Alexander, you told me there was a young boy he raised from the dead."

"Yes," he said. "It was the young son of a widow."

Simon nodded.

Alexander continued. "And there was another—a girl. We were told not to speak of it, but I suppose now it is acceptable to say. She is the daughter of a man named Jairus, in Galilee. She had passed days earlier, and Jesus commanded her to rise again."

Rufus then spoke. "I have heard in the streets that just before Jesus came to Jerusalem, there was another. A man who had been dead and buried for four days."

"But, Father," Alexander interrupted. "Jesus did these things himself. This time it is *he* who is dead. Can he raise himself?"

Simon looked down again and stirred the dirt.

"My son, my son . . ." His voice trailed off, and he looked up with moist eyes. "My dear son. It was you who had the courage to believe years before I did. It was you who was committed to leave your employ and follow him. You had the commitment to move your family. Alexander, were it not for you, I would not be here today. I would be lost in my own doubts and disbeliefs. But *you* showed me what it is to believe. This morning, when you returned with the news that he had risen, you could barely talk through your excitement."

Simon looked at his son with compassion and went on. "But, my son, whom I honor, when you just now weighed our worldly understanding against what has happened, you let doubt confront you and give you pause. Alexander, you—we—need to hold fast to what we know. This will not be the first time the world will challenge us."

"You are saying we need to remember what he did when he was here?" Alexander said. "To remember the miracles."

A tear rolled down Simon's cheek. "Yes, I am saying *remember*, but I am saying something more important than that. Whether he ever performed miracles or not, whether he ever raised someone from the dead or not, I *know* he is risen because he told us he would rise. And I believe what he says . . ."

Simon's voice cracked. "I believe because I know, and I know because here, in my heart, he has testified to me of the truth. And now I need nothing else except the knowledge of what he needs me to do for him. And when I know that, I will do it."

Simon looked at the faces of his family, pausing on each one to smile and look them in the eye, eventually resting his gaze on Alexander. "This is what I believe about our Savior, which I know to be true. It is not that I feel it, it is that I *know* it, as I know my own name. He is the Son of God as he has told us, and what he has taught us is true. I would sooner lay down my life than deny it."

No one spoke for a long time. It was a peaceful solitude, not awkward. There, in a courtyard in the middle of the Holy City, amidst a little huddle of believers who had witnessed both the death and resurrection of the Savior, the Spirit descended upon them, affirming the things Simon told them.

In searching for words to describe it, Alexander would later say, "It came upon us like a dove."

The following morning, Alexander arose and heard his father out in the courtyard. He walked out to find Simon packing the donkeys.

"You are ready to leave?" Alexander asked as he patted his father on the back.

Simon looked at him as he was closing one of the bags. "I am."

"Where are you going—back to Cyrene?"

"Perhaps so. Perhaps not."

Alexander looked quizzically at him.

Simon stood up and patted the donkey. "Do you remember when you first came back home after hearing Jesus? Do you remember what you told us?"

"Well, I told you a great deal. There was so much that had happened. Which part do you mean?"

"The part about the fishermen. You told us that the Savior approached them and, as I recall, he asked them to leave their nets and follow him, and just like that, they did it."

Simon laughed. "You looked at us all and, wide-eyed, said, 'Just like that, they followed him!'"

Alexander shook his head as he remembered. "Yes, it was Peter, the one who stood first and washed his hands and started walking. Then Andrew, James, and John."

"Well," Simon said, looking him in the eye. "If the Messiah will accept a lowly fisherman, perhaps he will accept a lowly merchant. I am leaving my nets, and I am ready to follow him."

"And I."

Both men turned to see Mara coming up behind them. "We are all ready, my faithful husband."

Soon thereafter, the small caravan of Simon's family left the home of Eber and stepped out into the world. They walked forward, unsure where their next steps would take them but absolutely certain that if that was where Jesus wanted them to go, they would go there and do what they could to spread the word.

Over the coming years, Simon and his sons would join with Paul and traverse the Roman Empire, teaching the word of God wherever anyone would listen. And whenever they encountered the poor, the brokenhearted, the blind, or the captive in spirit, the faithful and humble man of Cyrene—the man who had silently born the cross for his Savior—would share his food, offer his cloak, and preach good tidings, telling his own story and teaching them the way of truth.

Acknowledgments

First of all, thanks to all those who have helped me realize my dreams—from my mother, who listened to all my stories I wrote in crayon, to Warren Allen Smith, my high school English teacher, who made me write . . . and write . . . and write. Thanks to all the wonderful people at Ensign Peak: Lisa Mangum and Janna DeVore, who were assigned the unenviable task of editing my work; Richard Erickson and his team of designers, who were brilliant in their work on the cover; Rachael Ward, for her typesetting skills; and so many others I have not met but who had a hand in the many steps of bringing books to life. Special thanks to Chris Schoebinger, who took a chance on me.

Second, thanks to Loree, who has encouraged me to pursue this writing dream from our beginning. She saw more, and sees more, in me than I can see myself and has been my partner in working to make it come to pass. In addition, she has shown me what a true relationship with the Savior can be. While she has taught me a great deal about the gospel of Jesus Christ, the best thing she does is live it, richly, in every area of her life.

Finally, I would like to thank Him, as I do every day of my life, for breath, for direction, for forgiveness, and for hope.